THE SEAMOUNT STORIES

The Seamount Stories

Tony Martello

BROKEN TRIBE PRESS

The Seamount Stories

Cover art and design by Jacob Arms

Published by Broken Tribe Press
Lawrence Landing Company
Raleigh, North Carolina 27609
USA, North America

Broken Tribe Press is a proud member of:

Independent Book Publishers Association
 and
Community of Literary Magazines and Presses

www.brokentribepress.com

BROKEN TRIBE PRESS

CONTENTS

BY LAND OR SEA?

The couple lands at the Kona International Airport. Taylor has a plan to propose to his girlfriend of eight months. He knows he must take her to the hottest place on earth where neither lover has been before. This one is not like his first wife who hounded him daily for leaving shoes in the entryway and pressured him to climb the corporate ladder to no avail.

As they exit the stairs from Aloha Airlines, Taylor dreams, "This one is more like *Pele* whose veins warm the earth to her core, whose arms embrace me with molten magma, and whose fingers steam at the touch of the Pacific waters!" They proceed to the baggage claim and retrieve their suitcases. Taylor leads them to a long line for a rental car. He walks over to the marketing pamphlets stacked up against the wall where visitors search for tourist attractions and endless activities. He grabs a thick pamphlet and takes it to his girlfriend, "Lana, since we're going to be here for a few days, try and find a few activities for us. I'm going to check on getting a Cherokee" While Lana browses the tracts, Taylor walks around the corner where he can't be overheard. He approaches a local guy behind the desk of the jeep rental line, "Hey, I have a question for you. I want to take my lady to the place where the lava flows to the ocean. "The local guy replies, "Ah, you mean Kilauea, where da lava flows in the ocean by Kalapana, or into Kapoho Bay?" Taylor's eyes widen, "yeah, I think that's the spot. The desk clerk continues, "Da way I see it, brah, is you can go by land, or you can go by sea." Taylor's right eye squints upward, "I see, what is the hike like to get there by foot?" "Ho, brah, it's like a long two-mile hike and you get da *vog*... you know, da kine volcanic fog, it can get thick, and sting your eyes."

The local clerk warns, "Your lady not gone like da vog, braddah, you might try to go by boat and go down to Kalapana, and into Kapoho Bay, it's unreal, you gone blow her mind!" Taylor likes this idea and asks the clerk more questions, "Where do I go to sign up?" The local replies, "Try Lava Boat Trips," They have an aluminum boat and can take out like ten people per journey. It's unreal."

What would you do? Weave through dangerous billows of volcanic fog or brave the molten sea in an aluminum boat with boiling water surrounding you?

Taylor envisioned them walking across super-hot lava rocks while the soles of their shoes melt, sticking to the rugged terrain. Lana may like the tactile touch of the young hot earth but what about the catatonic smell of sulfuric acid sizzling all around her? On the other hand, she may appreciate a romantic boat ride along the wild and unpredictable Kalapana coastline. Whichever way he chose would have its drawbacks. The boat ride seemed scarier with the potential of getting lost at sea or capsizing, but the smoky hike seemed harsh and uncomfortable. If anyone could handle hiking in the *vog*, it was Lana, as she had been in many fires in both houses and dry land. She had been working as a firefighter for fifteen years in which five of those were fighting wildland California state fires. She was obsessed with fire-its bright color, mystery, and power. Because of her experience managing fire and its destructive effects, Taylor had to top it-he had to present her with the ultimate fire experience. Taylor knew that he must be comfortable if he was going to ask this woman to marry him, so he chose the boat trip and called to schedule a Lava Boat tour for day number two of their getaway. He returned to his fiancé standing in line. "Lana, pick an activity tomorrow because I have plans for us on Thursday." Her curiosity peaked, "Sounds mysterious. I've been reading about the Humuhumu triggerfish that can swim through hot water and warm vents. Have you heard of that one?" Taylor laughs, "Humu-humu-unuku-unuku-apuaa. It's the Hawaii state fish."

Lana chuckles, "I read an interesting legend about how this fish represented a Hawaiian leader who was piglike, had a snout and was sneaky in his shape-shifting ways. One day he met Pele in all her fiery boldness. She had steam billowing off her hair and the water around her was boiling to the touch. He fell in love with her and asked her to marry him. Soon thereafter, she realized he was too piglike and snidely, so she condemned him to the underworld where he turned into a colorful triggerfish that roams the islands today." At this moment Taylor knew he made the right decision to propose via boat ride. Now, he must figure out how to deliver the proposal and put the ring on her finger.

How would you do it?

That morning they wake up early and brew some Kona coffee. They scoop up some papaya with granola and yogurt and a squirt of lemon and enjoyed a nice breakfast. On the way to Pahoa, they stop and swim in the volcanic pools nestled in the lava rocks. They arrive at the park where the boat ride begins. The captain is hosing down his boat and checking all the parts to make sure it is in full working condition. Lana tells Taylor, "I'm going to use the bathroom." She walks over to the restrooms.

Taylor seizes an opportunity to ask the captain about an idea he has. "Hey captain, we are scheduled to go on a boat ride with you at 7:00 pm, I am wondering how I can surprise my girlfriend with a marriage proposal on the ride?" The salt-crusted man in his late forties drops the hose and smiles...I got one for you brah that will blow her mind. I have always wanted someone to be brave enough to try it but have had no takers."

Taylor steps closer blazing with curiosity, "Tell me more!" The captain chuckles a bit and says, ok, I must reveal one of our surprises that you may like for your proposal..., you promise not to tell anyone aboard the ship? Taylor obliges, "for sure, captain." The captain continues, "we dip a bucket into the 120-degree ocean water and pull it up for our tourists to feel once we get to the lava pouring in the ocean." Taylor leans in closer, and the captain suggests, "I will drop the ring in the bucket after I pull it from the ocean, but you must encourage your girlfriend to be the volunteer to test the waters if you will?" Taylor agrees, "she will for sure. She is brave and adventuresome. Oh, no, here she comes." Taylor hands the captain the ring, the captain nods agreeing to a plan that will seal Taylor's fate in marriage.

The boat launches at 7:00 under a starry night sky. The tour motors up and down over the vast ocean next to the largest mountains in the world if you measure it from the seafloor to the top of the island. Taylor and Lana gaze at the sky and sea when they notice a large ember-like vein slithering into the ocean. Steam sizzles above the glowing orange vein flowing from the landmass of Hawaii. As the boat approaches the lava flowing into the ocean the captain announces, "We are going to drift here for a while, who would like to test the waters for us and do a temperature check?" The captain slyly reaches into his pocket while the deckhand is dropping the bucket into the water when suddenly Taylor spots the ring flying across the boat deck and hears a small thud. He jumps to pick it up and raises his hand to volunteer all in one fell swoop. "Wow, it feels like a hot jacuzzi, wait, what is this? I feel a rock in here!" Taylor lifts the ring out of the water and holds it up, "Lana, will you marry me?" The crew cheers and Lana says, "yes" but Taylor can't hear her under the roar of the crowd!

AROUND THE WALL

"Hugo, what's that on your face?" asks Daniel as he looks a little closer. Hugo sits upon the canvas bag he was sleeping on last night. Paz reaches over and peels the piece of rough fabric off his cheek. "Wow!" she responds. "You have a tattoo of this miserable place right on your cheek." A small grid remains imprinted on his cheek. "It may be miserable, but it kept us alive another night," Daniel proclaims so the rest can hear.

Paz sniffs the air, "Do you smell that...like damp fish."

"Damp, fish? What is damp fish?" Hugo asks sarcastically. "Aren't all fish wet?" he continues.

"But, it's kind of old and crusty," Daniel confirms. "The damp you smell could be the fog." Slivers of soft grey light slip through the cracks of the rusty rooftop. The corners of the eaves are open as if the reinforcements rusted away from the edges of the dilapidated structure. This edifice could collapse any second.

Daniel points to the canvas bags, "And, those are probably the bags they use for distribution."

One of the younger kids asks, "What is dee-stra-buh-shun?"

"Isn't that how they send out the fish to the stores?"

Paz asks Daniel.

"*Si*," Daniel responds confidently. He is wearing a red and black flannel shirt with designs that resemble the imprint on Hugo's cheek. He kicks open one of the doors to the back alley of the warehouse. The sprouts of black hair on his chin and cheekbones give him the authority to lead the caravanners. The group rushes out to see them.

Last night they fled the *Ciudad de Tijuana* and found this abandoned warehouse near the beach. Some of the teens file out into the alley when Daniel calls them back in, "Not yet, we must see where we are before we all go." One of the youngsters in the group pleads, "I'm hungry. what are we doing for food, today?" Paz reaches over and puts her tranquil hand on him and says, "We got it: Daniel and I will go on a hunt, but I want you to collect those large, shimmering shells for me, and make a *palapa* with those canvas bags. When we are gone, others will know we survived and took refuge here in this abandoned fish cannery." The child agrees and Paz walks over to Daniel.

"Hugo, keep an eye on everyone while Paz and I go look for food."

"For sure, boss. I won't let anybody out, and I'll be on the lookout while you guys are gone."

"Paz, come with me. Let's go see what we can find across the alley by the beach." She nods and follows Daniel. Paz's normally long and lustrous black hair bounces with knots and tangles the size of her fists. Daniel remembers how her beautiful hair used to cascade down to the curve of her lower back before they began their trek to freedom and opportunity. The big knots in her hair reminds him of the ugly challenges and lost lives they have endured so far. He relishes those memories of playing in the coffee fields back home and chasing Paz down to the Lake Atitlan. They would swim in the water for hours and then raid the coffee plantations for bright red cherries and then dip them in his *abuela's mole* sauce for fun. One day, Daniel took Paz to the butterfly grove nearby and kissed her on the lips. To this day, she hasn't said whether they are boyfriend and girlfriend, but he has believed it ever since that day.

As the teens walk down the alley, Paz stops quietly, "Daniel, listen to the calling of the waves. It sounds a little bit like Acapulco when we camped on the beach."

"I know, I just couldn't get Pilon out of my head since he fell from the truck on the highway."

It has been three weeks since the caravan stopped in Acapulco along their journey. Daniel slows his speech, "Do you think those waves can show us the way? They are louder and more promising than those lapping wind waves in Lake Atitlan." Paz smiles, "Yes, and we don't have to hear the buzzing of fishing boats looking for bass. Follow me, Daniel, I see a light on in that silver shack near the dunes." She clenches his hand and pulls him onto the damp sand, a much colder and more mysterious feel than the warm, granular grains in Acapulco. A tiny bit of blue light turns orange with rays breaking the horizon. "I smell coffee" Paz exclaims. "Follow your nose" Daniel encourages. They step up on a cement slab that goes for yards down the beach. Daniel takes the lead and walks up to the side of the tin shack. Paz shuffles beside him. Daniel peers his head into the front and notices two young men in their twenties. One has blond wavy hair and the other has black matted hair that appears to stick to his forehead. They hunch over a wooden cutting board and are chopping the heads off small baitfish. "Ahh, fish and coffee, I don't know if they go together," Paz laughs. Daniel gives a courtesy laugh and responds vehemently, "At this point, the gang would take fish in their coffee!" Paz's brilliant white teeth show, "You're right, patron! Let's see if those guys can help us. They look like fishermen. Maybe they can be *fishers of men...and women*, of course?" "Good one," Daniel replies.

Paz steps up to the outside counter, "Hola, can you guys spare some coffee and a pack of tortillas?" The boy with the black hair responds, "Oh, we open in fifteen minutes. What kind of bait would you like?" Daniel and Paz turn to each other for a brief second and then Paz replies, "We are not fishing this morning, we are looking for food and water for our crew. We got stranded here after escaping the *Federales* last night. Two of our friends got stabbed in Tijuana for taking grub from the food trucks. We tried to help them but the *Federales* showed up and we fled to this area." The young man with the blond hair turns to Paz and stares into her eyes. He is allured with the golden hue around her iris' and even with her messy hair and plain black sweater, her beauty radiates like beacons in the night to the young fishermen. "Wow, your eyes sparkle like the scales of a dorado!" Paz smiles. Daniel interrupts furiously, "Our gang is thirsty, hungry, and could use some tortillas. Could you guys spare a couple dozen or so?"

The boy with the black hair shakes his head side to side, "I'm sorry, but my father would not approve of me giving away food from the bait shack. You guys must go."

"Wait one second, Thomas," the blond man suggests. "Where are you guys headed?"

"Coronado del Rey" Paz answers.

Thomas says, "You mean San Diego, right? Taylor, I think she is talking about San Diego."

Taylor shares, "I used to live specifically in Coronado Del Rey, there, when I was ten-years old. It is a beloved vacation place for kings and presidents. I loved it, I used to surf there every day and eat fish tacos and play volleyball on the beach. The waves are glassy there and the sunsets are amazing!"

Paz replies, "Sounds nice but we heard they have jobs there maintaining a large estate. We need jobs."

"Taylor, I think they are planning on crossing the wall at the border."

"Yeah, well, I can't blame them, I had many good times there."

"Taylor, get back to cutting the bait and I will take care of them."

Before Taylor walks back over to the chopping block, Paz bends over and reaches down into her sock. A brilliant tattoo of a monarch butterfly floats above her lower back like a hologram. Taylor and Thomas both gaze in amazement at the symbolic creature and marvel at the beautiful girl in their midst. Days and days of fishing have a way of beating the beauty right out of you, and this new visitor is a refreshing sight to see. Paz continues to reach deep into her grey sock and pulls out a large black pearl the size of a grape.

"Dios Mio!" Thomas cries. The others raise their eyebrows in wonder as well.

The boys pause for a second....

"If you guys take *mi Novio* and I, along with our gang across the border, I will give you this monstrous black pearl. It has to be worth at least fifty thousand *pesos*."

Daniel lifts his chest, puts his arm around his confirmed girlfriend, and adds in, "and...p*or favor*...can you throw in two dozen tortillas and anchovies so we can feed our crew. we have four others caravanning with us." Sun rays break through the clouds announcing morning-time and Daniel welcomes it with a boost of confidence.

Thomas clenches a fish dagger and commands, "Hand over that pearl, or I'll call the *Federales*!" Daniel shuffles his stance to turn toward Thomas while protecting Paz and asks Thomas an enterprising question, "Why would you do that when you can potentially have fifty thousand *pesos* and maybe even more if we tell you where the other pearls are after you help us across the wall?"

"You mean *around* the wall" Taylor interjects. "We are not thieves but fishermen, Thomas, like your father taught us. We help provide sustenance and hope for the village. The sea is full of surprises, and miracles happen every day right in front of our eyes. Can't you see it? Don't you want to be part of it?"

"But I can't risk everything, my dad's business, our jobs," Thomas worries.

Taylor slides closer to the young couple and in between Thomas and them. "I will take them around the wall in the dinghy boat, so you don't have to risk anything, and you can buy the bigger aluminum boat you always wanted with the money from that pearl."

Thomas releases the dagger and relaxes his shoulders but comes up with more dubious questions. "How do you think you'll motor them *around* the wall? Are you crazy?"

"I will cruise the path between the Mexican Navy ships and the San Diego border patrol."

Thomas continues, "Both parties can see everything, and they will find you guys, they have radar and marine hovercraft boats all over the place."

Taylor smiles, "but, there is a brief time where we stand a better chance—*coffee time*—during the thick fog between five and six a.m. and the shift change of night into day. It is June gloom weather now and we have *Dios* on our side."

Paz opens the palm of her hand, exposing the glistening black and purple hue of the pearl. She considers the days, weeks, and months the oyster had to endure this abrasive grain of sand stuck in its soft tissue. How is it that this chronic irritation could create such beauty and pay-off at such a high rate? Maybe miracles can happen and in many mysterious ways, through suffering, opportunity, and faith. She hoped for this for her and the crew.

"Do we have a deal?" Paz entices.

Thomas leans against the wooden chopping board, takes a slow breath, and replies, "Ok, but you must tell me where the other pearls are now."

Daniel asserts, "No, we will give you the pearl when we launch the boat for our escape and will tell Taylor where the other treasures are for his return. Then you can make plans to buy your own company." Thomas' eyes peer up as if dreaming up a big opportunity.

"Ok, Deal," Thomas agrees.

"Meet us here early tomorrow at 5:00 a.m. sharp. I will have the boat ready with water, crackers, and life jackets," Taylor assures.

Paz squeezes her palm, covering the valuable reward, and slides it back into her other sock. Daniel reminds Thomas of his extra request, "Oh, and could you still share with us with tortillas and anchovies? We would appreciate it."

Thomas walks to the bait freezer and takes out two small bundles of frozen fish and two packs of tortillas.

"Gracias," Daniel thanks him confidently.

Paz and Daniel walk back through the alley with the life-saving sustenance Taylor referred to earlier in their conversation. Daniel turns to Paz, "Mi mariposa, you never stop amazing me. I had no idea you found that incredible pearl. Where did you acquire that rare treasure?"

"On the beach in Acapulco, when I wanted to be alone with you. I took a walk to get away from the crew for a few minutes and found it in the sand near a tourist palapa down the beach."

Paz nestles into Daniel's arm, "I kept if for something special, and if this doesn't qualify, I don't know what does."

"Well, this qualifies. I'm happy you found it. Let's get back to the crew and prepare them for the grand escape."

The couple is greeted with eager faces and hungry mouths as the kids jump up and down when they see the food. Daniel asks Hugo, "Can you divvy up these tortillas and anchovies and make sure the others get a couple wraps each?" Hugo laughs, "*Si, patron*! Fish don't last long before it goes bad." Hugo parses them out for the gang. They place the anchovies in the sunlight shining through the rusty windows to thaw them out, then roll them up in tortillas and scarf them down quickly. Then, they find an old crusty faucet with running water and take turns drinking to wash down the salty brine from their fish wraps.

Paz eats with the other girls and Hugo approaches Daniel. "Hey Daniel, how was your time alone with Paz?" Hugo's chubby cheeks wait in anticipation of exciting news. "It was an adventure, *amigo*. She called me her boyfriend right in front of the two fishermen." Hugo's dark, beady eyes open larger than Paz's black pearl. "And, what next, boss? Did you kiss her?"

"No, it wasn't the right time. We were in serious discussions about sustenance and escape!"

"Sounds exciting, Daniel"

"They are helping us escape, *amigo*! First thing tomorrow morning, we wake up and go on their boat into freedom!" Daniel shares the news with his friend and realizes he must lead effectively. He has an official girlfriend now and is the oldest and strongest. He must tell the whole gang, so they understand their part in the grand escape to America.

"Gather around everyone, we have a chance to get help to make it across the border. We must lie low here today and stay another night so we can get up early in the dark and get on a boat to cross the border into America." All four youngsters lean in and listen. Paz puts her arm around the youngest girl. She anticipates the girl's response, "But, I have never been on a boat, and I don't know how to swim."

"Don't worry, *prima*, they have life jackets for us to keep us afloat if we have to go in the water, but we will be in the boat the whole way to San Diego."

The other boy who built his palapa says, "I spent the last hour creating my beach shack, *el Grande*. Look, you guys like it?"

Hugo jumps in, "I want it, can I use it as a model to build my house when I get across the border?" The boy laughs and the gang returns to their spots in the cold cannery. The gang spends the rest of the day chatting about their mysterious future that lies in the hopeful hands of the fishermen they barely know.

The next morning the cannery crew wakes at 4:00 am to thick, brisk fog. Paz checks to make sure her prized pearl is still in her presence. Thankfully, it is, and she is relieved that they didn't disclose where they were sheltering for the night. Daniel gathers the group and has them funnel through the alley out onto the cement slab near the dunes. As the remaining caravanners get close to the bait and tackle shop, Paz lifts her nose, "Smell that coffee, Daniel? Let's get a cup for the ride if they let us."

They arrive at the silvery shop. It is beaded with thick condensation and permeates with the smell of sardines. Taylor is out front with a wooden dinghy twenty feet long and eight feet wide. He is wearing black board shorts and a grey Quicksilver T-shirt. The young girl that was worried about boats and swimming notices a blue shark imprinted on Taylor's shirt; its jaws are wide open and jumping right off the shirt in a three-dimensional spiral. She asks Paz, "there aren't sharks out here are there?"

"No worries, Nina, the big ones are way out by the Mexican navy ships. We only have baby ones here in the shallows." Taylor chuckles and continues, "They nibble on my toes when I forget to clip my nails, ha, ha." The whole gang laughs, and Taylor reaches into a cooler to grab a box of crackers and bottled water.

"Each of you gets your own bottled water and can chew on these saltine crackers if you want. Oh, and everyone goes to the bathroom in the back before boarding the *S. S. Taylor*."

Thomas stands quietly under the tin roof by the shop. He watches Paz tend to the children and remains quiet for the time being. "Thomas, where are the black life preservers?" Taylor asks. "They are in the old wood tackle box in the back. Just don't give them the orange ones or you may be spotted," Thomas reminds Taylor. Taylor fits the black life preservers on the six caravanners and carries on preparing without wearing one himself.

Daniel asks Taylor, "How long of a boat ride is this to San Diego?" Well, it normally would be just twenty-five to thirty minutes, but I'm taking you north of Field State Beach which may take up to an hour, hour-and-half or so. We must navigate beyond the border patrol closer to shore and ride the buffer between the navy ships farther out to sea and the shoreline sand patrol. Once we make it to the safe zone north of there, you guys are free to head up to Coronado del Rey. I have a contact there for you who'll help you with a place to stay and get settled." Daniel's eyes focus on curiosity. "Why are you being so nice, and risking your job for us?" Taylor replies with enthusiasm, "You are the brave ones. I would gladly help your gang find freedom—it is worth fighting for. How far have you traveled with your group?" Daniel's head drops a bit, "from Guatemala and we lost four on the way."

"My condolences. I will pray we deliver your crew safely and with hope!"

Thomas walks over to the boat near the shore, "May I have the pearl?"

Paz takes the pearl out of her pocket and hands it to Thomas, "Here you go. Thank you for helping us. Good luck on finding your new aluminum boat."

He takes the pearl and walks back to his shop. Taylor motions to have everyone climb in the boat. He slowly tugs the boat, getting it afloat in the shallow water. "Jump in everyone, we must leave, it's 4:45 am." The four youngsters get in first, then Paz, and then Daniel. Daniel nods to Taylor that his group is ready to go.

As they motor over the waves and out past the breakers, Taylor warns them they may have to hit the deck if they see any navy ships or border hovercraft. "If I motion down with both my hands, just hit the deck so other boats can't see you guys, Ok?" The gang nods and listens with astute ears. "The idea here is to make it look like there are only one or two fishermen in the boat. Let's say Daniel and I can be seen but the rest of you have to duck when other vessels cruise by." There are two paddles and a fishing rod stored under the rails of the boat. Taylor encourages Hugo to try the rod, "Hugo, get one of those anchovies out of the cooler, take the rod, and hook it deep into the mouth...I'll show you how to cast it."

"Ooo, damp fish again," Hugo chuckles. He takes the bait and places the hook from the rod and line into the anchovies' mouth.

Taylor checks, "Looks good." He swings the pole back, holding his finger on the rod and line, then releases. The dead baitfish flies above everyone's head and lands out beyond the stern of the dinghy. "Let that bait ride, and we may get a hot tuna on the line." Hugo's eyes bounce as he laughs and watches in amazement.

Trolling north, and twenty minutes into the escape, Taylor glances right to gauge the location of the wall and border area. In contrast to the intimidating and highly enforced wall on land, a few hundred yards from the sea, the wall looks like nothing more than an ill-fated attempt to scare away swimmers, surfers, and random wanderers from crossing the imaginary border under the surface of the water. In Taylor's mind, the sea is fair game and owned only by *Dios* on high. No human has the right to control lines at the bottom of the sandy sea. As a surfer and fisherman, he understands the universal truth that a sea is a place of freedom and open to all. Sharing it with these brave migrants makes him feel empowered and connected to the rest of the world.

"Daniel, *mira!*" Hugo shouts. Suddenly a brilliant golden fish about five-feet long jumps over the bow of the S. S. Taylor.

The skipper grabs the rod and hands it to Hugo, "Reel her in Hugo, we have a dorado-on" Hugo huffs and puffs as he reels the rod vigorously. The kids jump up and down with excitement cheering, "*Vamos, primo, Vamos, primo!*" After fifteen minutes of tugging, relaxing, and reeling, Hugo brings the dorado aboard. Shimmering hues of iridescent blues, greens, and gold float on the scales like a rainbow. Daniel glances at Paz and sees the resemblance in her eyes. Taylor was right, this fish is beautiful!

Taylor asks one of the younger boys to steer the boat while he begins gutting the fish for fresh sushi. "Keep your eyes open that way! And don't turn right!" While Taylor is gutting the dorado, a huge shark jumps onto the stern about a foot from the motor.

The younger girl screams, "*Tiburon*, just like on Taylor's shirt."

Suddenly, Daniel reaches under the side rail, whisks out a paddle, and slaps the shark right on its nose. It dives back into the water and swims away.

Paz pulls the girl back and marvels at her long-time friend, "*Mi novio, no puedo creerlo!*"

Taylor smiles and exclaims, "Daniel, you saved the day! That was a mako, the fastest shark in the ocean." The caravanners cheer in excitement. Taylor finishes carving up the dorado and serves slices of fresh sushi to the passengers. They are delighted with the sweet taste of the sea, so they snack on saltine crackers and drink the bottled water. Taylor glances right again and realizes he has officially made it around the wall but keeps it to himself. As he approaches the north end of Field State Beach, a hovercraft buzzes toward him smoothly across the surface of the San Diego shoreline. He motions for the passengers to duck and has Hugo act as a decoy, or rather, an experienced fisherman, now. The border patrol-craft cruises about thirty yards in front of them peering over to the *S. S Taylor*. Taylor nods and holds up their catch sort of showing off but indicating they were just fishing. The skipper of the patrol nods and the caravanners carry on north for another ten minutes.

"Okay, guys. I have a friend, Antonio, who is meeting us on the beach. He will take you to the estate of Coronado Del Rey and then connect you with the groundskeeper to see if he can help you find your contact and find work for you." Taylor steers the boat closer to shore and docks in the sand near a small harbor. There is no border patrol in sight. They all climb out of the dinghy. Paz kisses Daniel on the lips and Hugo yells, "Ah, *novio!*" and the passengers walk with Taylor to the edge of the harbor. "Welcome to America!" Taylor exclaims. He introduces them to Antonio and returns to his boat. On his way back to Baja, he lifts his hand off the steering wheel and prays in Spanish: "*Gracias, Dios Mio,*" entirely forgetting to ask where the rest of the pearls are.

BENEATH THE SHADES

Every summer a select group of students from Stanford University comes to Fallen Leaf Lake to camp out, row, and water ski the glassy lake of privilege. The lake is so glassy that Randy can see her reflection as she steps into his kayak. The glow of her blond hair reverberates off the water like a radiant beacon warning him of her rocky shores. The sequins on her black two-piece sparkle, emitting interstellar messages from her bikini onto the water surface-reflecting back through his polarized sunglasses. These signals indicate she is an important young woman with status. As Rhonda steps in, the kayak sinks slightly. The first thing Randy notices isn't her eyes but her pink and black *Prada* sunglasses. Randy recalls purchasing his *Prizm* Oakley's because they were polarized and able to see into the depths of the water. He must keep an eye out for rocks, branches, and shallow dangers while steering the boat for his customers.

"Is this boat safe? She asks.

"One of the safest unless you rock it, of course. The Blue Dolphin 1000 is very stable and can float eight people. I know it's named after a majestic ocean creature, but it'll do fine here in a serene lake"

"I dig your pink sunglasses," Randy jokes.

"Thank you. I bought them at Nieman Marcus while shopping in New York. I was visiting my cousin who just graduated from Cornell University this spring. She's going to law school this fall. She got into Harvard Law."

"Congratulations, she'll be swimming in stacks of paper deeper than this lake. No, just kidding, that's a huge accomplishment," Randy slips sarcastically.

Rhonda sits on the wooden bench and clenches onto the side of the fiberglass rail. As she squeezes the side of the kayak she asks, "Can you paddle me over to the south side of the lake? I want to meet up with my girlfriends and bring them back to camp."

Randy paddles several strokes. Rhonda gazes upon Randy's triangular triceps as he proudly transports the goddess across the lake of privilege. There is virtually no wind and visibility are excellent on the horizon. The water is exceptionally clear today. Randy continues to paddle closer to the rugged shore where grey-green slabs of mountainous rock cascade into the crystal water. Rhonda keeps a tight hold of the boat rail. Randy tries to focus on the task at hand but his imagination drifts into the glam and glory of his prestigious customer.

"Hey, look over there on that rock," he points.

Rhonda grabs the left corner of her sunglasses, lowering them onto her nose. Her green eyes escape the shade and seem to float on her tan skin. Their color matches one of the deeper shades of green in Emerald Bay.

"Oh my God, is that a bear?"

"Yep, a California Black Bear. What a beauty!"

Rhonda slides over to Randy and clenches his arm.

She hangs on him tightly and demands, "No, please take me more to the middle. I don't want to hit the shore and get anywhere near that bear!"

Randy chuckles and obliges. He paddles back out into the deeper blue depths toward the middle of the lake. He is amused at her nervous uncertainty and enjoys her need to cling to him for strength and security. "My father has a bear on the emblem above his desk office in Sacramento. It's in the California State Assembly seal."

"Ah, the California state animal, the Grizzly. Thankfully, these bears are smaller- California black bears."

Rhonda searches to the south and asks Randy to row her past Emerald Bay near the dock so she can meet her friends.

As they pass Emerald Island, he skirts the shallows and asks Rhonda, "You like to fish, want to throw a line out? There are usually rainbow trout circling the island."

"Sure, I like the rainbow colors, I just don't want scales sticking to my nail polish."

Randy loads his hook with pink salmon eggs and lets a line out off the end of the boat.

Rhonda keeps her eyes focused on the southern shores past the island when suddenly, the boat tugs slightly. Randy shuffles to the back of the boat and pulls up something much heavier than a rainbow trout- it's a dead human body with bluish-grey skin and a bloated face with no eyes. The fish must have eaten the eyes out of the sockets.

Randy quickly cuts the line before Rhonda has a chance to see the body sink back down to the bottom. He leaves a line out while they paddle closer to shore.

"Okay, we're just about there," he transitions.

"Thank you, Randy. How do I get a hold of you if I need another ride?"

"Just dial 1-530-222-7777, and I'll come and get you!"

"Thanks for the adventure, I'll be sure to give you a call when I return."

On his way back, Randy curiously marveled at how deep his shades could penetrate and wondered what he would see next.

MALADY MAHI

I used to wonder why I wouldn't get seasick on my surfboard but every time I took a boat ride outside the bay, I would turn whiter than any midwestern tourist on his first day of vacation in Hawaii. I would desperately attempt to focus on the horizon with that salty sailor confidence that Ralph had but would eventually hurl over the side, feeding the South Pacific fish the wrong kind of food. Ralph didn't need badges-his nautical smile and the wrinkles on his skin spoke of many journeys out to sea. His stories, however, were out of this world. Whenever my mom would announce that she would be cooking chicken enchiladas with both Verde and red sauce, Ralph was there, and he would bring along an exciting adventure each time he came for dinner.

One time, he told us about how he was spearfishing for parrotfish on the south side of Kauai when a Tiger Shark circled above him. He had a big belt around his waist where he kept his netted catch. While diving for more fish, the shark must have sensed his catch and began to follow Ralph. He enacted how he had to unleash his belt and decoy the shark about thirty feet away from him and then swim up for a quick gulp of air and then dive back down below the reef to hide from the shark. He kept us hanging on edge by dramatically repeating his dive from the surface to the reef three times while the shark circled above him. We couldn't believe how he survived these encounters.

Another time, he blew our minds when he told us how he took his charter boat out with some guests when one tourist expected that he was catching a fish when he realized he had hooked into a piece of giant squid that had triangular Megalodon size teeth marks around it. He said the points of the teeth imprints were eight inches apart. His smile glistened large and mysterious, "There are no sharks anywhere, caught on record, with teeth that big," he told us, kids. We asked him several more questions like, "Did you ever see the giant squid? Or What was the biggest shark you ever saw?" Not only was he a real fisherman with the most exciting stories, but he was also a stylish surfer, too. So, as you can imagine, Ralph was my hero because he could *hang ten in the barrel* and captivate us, kids, with the best fishing stories ever!

As I grew older, I began surfing along the lava cliffs where big black, jagged chunks of the old extinct volcano were sprinkled across the reef. The comfort of my surfboard between me and the razor-sharp coral made me feel a little protected, but I always surveyed the surface and horizon for more danger. I paddled back out to the lineup where the waves would crest and roll across the reef like hollow glass cylinders. In between sets of waves, I sat still on my board and looked upon the lava cliff to the left of me, where a man, woman, and child were gazing over the cliff down into the foamy waves crashing against the rocks. I saw the adolescent throw something into the ocean. The family watched the object for about fifteen minutes and then left, walking back to their car. I caught a few more waves and then paddled into shore. While shuffling along the inside reef to get to the sand, I saw Ralph in his charter boat taking out another group of tourists to the Napali coast for spectacular views and exciting fishing.

I walk back to my truck and drive to *Hanalei Coffee Company* to finish my term paper. I ordered some extra dark Java and some banana-papaya pancakes and then dive into the last paper of the quarter. I spend close to three hours editing my Neuroscience project on the topic of the *mind-body interface.* I need to stretch and take a break, so I walk over to *The Island Grill* and order two mahi tacos with mango salsa. I walk back to my study station at the coffee shop and eat some lunch. Halfway into my second taco, Ralph strolls in with two of his tourists. They were beaming with radiant smiles like they just discovered El Dorado.

"Koni, you won't believe this one," Ralph sets me up for another fish story. But this is unusual because he doesn't normally bring his tourists to lunch or coffee. He pulls three chairs up to my table and invites the crew to have a seat with me.

"Koni, this is Diane from Chicago and Ken from Maui...Guys, this is Koni, he's a great surfer and he's getting his Masters in Neuroscience at the University of Hawaii." I smile and shake their hands, "Aloha, guys, welcome." I close my laptop and invite them to get comfortable.

"Ken, show Koni what you caught on our expedition today." Ken opens his bag and pulls out a small glass bottle with peeling red wax and a cork. There is a strip of white paper and a small single dose package of Advil ripped open.

Ralph looks at Diane and then me. "Diane, show Koni your keepsake."

Ralph's charter-guests put all the items on the table. Diane gently places a tiny gold coin on the table. I recognized the dull clanging of gold hitting the old wooden table.

"You guys found this floating in the sea?" I inquired further.

Ralph jumps in . . . "Even better," then Ken interrupts,

"It was in the belly of the mahi-mahi I caught!"

Ralph chuckles,

"You guys did hit El Dorado, that is if you are from Mexico because that is what a mahi-mahi is called in Mexico and California."

Ralph continues, "I asked Ken if he wanted to ship the mahi-mahi to Maui, but he decided to have me gut it and filet it for fresh sushi. When we opened the fish up, there was a *message in the bottle* right in the mahi's belly!" Never, have I seen anything like this before." This must have rocked Ralph's world because he wasn't the sentimental type. He was mysterious but not so sentimental. I enjoy seeing the master storyteller mystified himself.

There on the open table in front of me was a small glass bottle, a very tiny gold coin, an opened package of Advil, and a strip of paper with something handwritten on it. A curious thought began to rise from my short-term memory when Ralph reiterates,

"I have seen a lot of things in the stomachs of fish and sharks but never this. I've seen children's toys, glass fishing buoys, nets, hooks and more, but never this."

Then, I recall the family on the lava cliffs earlier today throwing something into the ocean. Could it have been this *message in a bottle* with these items? And, even more interesting, could the mahi-mahi have mistaken this to be a fish for a meal? I glance up at Ralph as his salt-crusted eyelids squint inward,

"Mahi go for surface bait. The fish may have mistaken this small glass bottle for a fish."

"Ralph, I saw a family of three earlier today throwing something the cliff at *Waikokos*.

Do you think it could have been this?"

"Possibly, and with the off-shore winds that picked up this afternoon, it could have blown out past the trolling lane where Ken caught the Mahi."

Meanwhile, Diane was stepping into the conversation and reached for the gold coin,

"Isn't this cute, I wonder if it's real? Ken, thanks for the gift, I feel like you should keep it since you caught the fish."

"No, I want you to have it after hearing about your busy life in Chicago and trying to find free time in your life, I feel like this may be a sign for you to contemplate." I asked to see the coin, "Can I see, wow, it looks like Jesus in the middle with a bunch of saints around him or apostles, and I see the date 2007." I pick up the coin and do an internet search.

My results show a 2007 Liberia-one fiftieth of an ounce-gold Thaler. It features a condensed snapshot of Christ's life with his face in the center surrounded by scenes of his birth, the last supper, and all the apostles with their names and faces. "Guys, this is like a message of faith in a lifetime right on one-fiftieth of an ounce on a gold coin. Spectacular, and Liberia means-*The land of Freedom*." Diane clenches the coin and puts it in her pocket. "I am so inspired by this. Thanks, Ken!"

I reach for the strip of paper that reads: *We hope this note finds you well and these items provide you with hope and relief to get you back on your given journey. When you make it to a computer with the internet, email us at surfersandhealers@gmail.com*

Ken stands up and hobbles a bit then shares, "I have been waiting to get a knee replacement for several years and was in a lot of pain this morning. Fighting that mahi took it out of me. My knee was killing me, so I took the Advil and will email this mystery person later." Ralph stands up and gathers his guests to go clean up. He prompts them, "Ok, guys, let's let Koni finish up his homework and head back to the boat to get your things." Diane and Ken both wish me luck on my paper and say, "Good-bye."

"Thank you for dropping by, nice to meet you guys. I hope the good luck continues," I encourage. On their way out, Ralph turns to me and slyly comments under his breath,

"Try putting that story in your *mind-body* paper, school-boy. And you can title it, "Malady Mahi"

DONKEY BEACH

Without any lifeguard training, we were going to Hawaii to save souls. *Who needed saving? Why were they in danger?* I wasn't so sure back then and all I did was imagine how much fun I could have on my orange and yellow spongey boogie board. I visualized a billowing sandy beach sprawled out amongst wispy pine trees and a small cove with peaky waves that broke left and right across the sand. With the scene imprinted in my imagination, I stood up on my *Orangesicle* bogey board, strapped the leash on my left wrist, and surfed it off my bed. I hit the ground hard and burned my right cheek into the old carpet. We were leaving in two weeks, and I would be ready!

The first time I felt sweat on my feet was when I stepped off the plane in Lihue. "Aloha, guys. Welcome to Kauai." The cheery red-faced pastor handed us small tracts of cartoon-like sketches of humans interacting in interesting and devious ways. I'll never forget the drawing of a man holding a bottle with an X on it. He had a dopy look on his face with bloodshot eyes and sat in a stupor on a barrel with more Xs on it. "I know of an unreal burger joint we can hit up on the way to Hanalei,

Ono char burger," Carey said.

We pull up to *Ono Char Burger*. It is an outdoor 60s burger joint scene with cement bench seats and pineapple-colored umbrellas polished over with firm fiberglass. Several chickens pecked around and under the tables as we slid over the hard cement benches and circled into an unplanned round table. I opened a tract that asked, "Have you been saved?" Below the title a disheveled man is bobbing on the surface of the ocean, reaching his hand out above the water, waiting for you, *the reader*, to clench his hand and pull him to shore, or maybe even your *lifeboat*.

"Try the aloha shake you guys, oh, and the loco boy burger, or teriyaki burger with pineapple," Carey encouraged.

Kauai had me at my first sip of the aloha shake. Even perplexed about this saving soul's business, it captured my taste buds with an explosion of mango juice combined with the exotic strawberry papaya and smoothed over with apple banana (small-kine) flavors. Put an X on this and I'll drink it any day. I flipped quickly through the tract and came to the last page where Jesus is in a lifeboat with flowing long brown hair, a tranquil white robe, and his last save- the man reaching out for help on the first page. My brother, Mike asked the pastor, "What are we saving them from?" The red-haired, jolly pastor smiled as his glasses tilted slightly to his right, "Sin, Michael, they have a fallen nature." *Who were they and why were they so bad?* Mike's eyes got a bit rounder and browner, "Oh, my, oh no..." I laughed inside because I knew my brother was responding sarcastically to an answer he didn't understand.

After experiencing what I consider to be one of the most paradoxical moments of my life, we got up from the round cement table and continued to drive to the north shore. Hundreds of mango trees shrouded the highway to Hanalei. Rows of yellow and iridescent hues of plumerias permeated the airways as we turned here and descended there. We passed the Kalihiwai river, and a screaming waterfall welcomed us to the north shore.

It wasn't until eight months later, at Donkey Beach, after we landed on Kauai, that I realized what we were here to do. Our mission was to save others from the snare of the devil, but I didn't like the approach, it was too *salesy. Why couldn't we invite them to save their own souls?* Maybe that would be nicer or more natural. In the last eight months, I learned how to surf warm water waves, share the word of God with others, and most importantly give waves to other surfers and tourists who came to visit Hawaii. Since we landed, we had bought false teeth for a struggling soul, we had housed several lost, homeless drifters, and saved many others from addiction and debauchery. I now know that the vision I had of the mysterious beach with wispy pine trees and swirly dunes turned out to be a real beach-*Donkey Beach*-where very few mainland tourists had ever visited.

THE PUT-BACK

Craig wakes up at 6:15 am to continue his technical treadmill of life. He carefully picks up his thick glasses, puts them on his narrow face, and rests them on his astute ears. His ears appear larger than average because of his short square salt and pepper cut. He reaches into his closet and chooses a beige, plaid collar shirt. He methodically dresses and marches into the kitchen to pour himself a cup of coffee for the road. He fills the silver and black thermos style mug and climbs into his white 2019 Toyota Prius hybrid. He drives to the highway 85 entrance and waits patiently in the single file line to get on the highway. His average wait per day is about 25 minutes. While in line, Craig reflects to a comment his coworker, John said the week earlier,

"Craig, all you have to do is just risk it and drive in the carpool lane, there aren't enough California Highway Patrol to catch everyone, and your odds are low that you will get caught and if they do get you- just pay the ticket. It's only $490 for greater peace of mind."

Craig tried not to cringe when John would rant on and on about his daily survival tactics. John is married with 2 kids and always talks his way out of trouble. John brags that he has been driving in the carpool lane for ten years and hasn't been caught. He estimates that he's saved about 1500 hours of time sitting in traffic in the last ten years. Craig would never take this risk. He was too calculated and careful to risk ruining his reputation and face the overwhelming embarrassment of getting a traffic ticket. Finally, Craig makes it to the main highway and glances at his Apple Watch. It shows that it took him 32 minutes to get on today.

While at work, Craig chats with John before their Quality meeting. John asks,

"Craig, how long did it take you to get in today?"

Craig sighs and responds, "an hour and 10 minutes. It took me 32 minutes to get on the highway today." John laughs. Dude, you need some excitement in your life. Have you ever had sushi? Craig shook his head side to side, "No, it isn't safe. I don't eat raw fish!"

John laughs again and insists, "meet me in the parking lot today at 11:45 am, I am taking you to sushi for lunch." Craig, feeling the pressure agrees, "Ok, but no raw fish."

Lunchtime rolls around, and the guys meet in the parking lot near John's silver Lexus CT200h. Craig slides into John's car and instantly notices more space and style than his simple white Prius. John encourages Craig, "Kick back and enjoy the ride, we need to unplug from the project for an hour and decompress. You know, creativity only comes with clarity, and we haven't had a second for ourselves to relax. Even Quality Engineers need some creative space occasionally."

Craig replies, "Ok, I just don't want to be late"

The coworkers pull up to Sushi Float, a local restaurant. John directs them over to the corner of the circular float. There are multiple sushi boats floating around the moat. They are linked together and have a variety of raw and cooked sushi assorted on them. John enlightens Craig, "These are rainbow rolls and have ahi, which is raw but there are others with cooked fish like the Unagi one with eel floating by."

John reaches out and grabs a rainbow roll tray with the raw ahi. Craig spots a boat approaching that has 2 round fried and battered golf ball sized appetizers. He reaches out and grabs it feeling more secure about the deep-fried morsels. John educates Craig, "Nice, you picked the fish balls!" Craig's eyes widen and his face tightens with fear. He anxiously returns the tray back on another sushi boat floating by. Craig comments further, "Dude, you did a Put-Back, you're not supposed to put a tray back once you take it off the boat, Shhh, don't say anything or we will have to pay for it." Craig still stunned replied, "I didn't know they had fish testicles here. I can't eat those." John let out a big laugh. "They're not really fish testicles. Fish don't have testicles; they are just called that. They are balls of rice cooked in deep fried batter."

The coworkers chose a few more trays and enjoy the rest of their meal. As they get up to leave, an attractive woman slides over and surprisingly introduces herself to Craig, "you are brave, I have never seen that pulled off. Here is my number. Call me."

JADE COVE

The cold-water stabs at Rico, penetrating his bones. Wind chops, bites, and claws at his face. The unfamiliar coastline of the Pacific digs out the survival in him. As he floats south with the currents, he drifts back to himself as a child of 12, treading the same trail every day to Don Hilario's vineyard. Back then, he found his endurance by listening to the melody of the ocean, but today, a much louder drum beat down on him:

crash, boom, roll
crash, boom, roll
crash, boom, roll

Just an hour ago, Rico was a shipmate aboard a vessel growing "the empire on which the sun never sets," and now, he found himself a castaway, among the ravaging waves of the sea, lost to fend for himself.

The day of the wreck was September 29, 1519, when the Castilian vessel, El Buscador ran adrift in the cold, misty fog en route to the Yucatan peninsula on a colonial mission for Spain. Rico and Alex, young lads in their early twenties, were commissioned to work on El Buscador, one of the ships assigned to the overseas expansion of Castile under royal authority by Spanish conquistadors.

Unlike today, the Lost Coast of old Mexico (California) had no lighthouses for ships, skirting the coast to the South in search of El Dorado. The ship smashed into the rocky Willow Point, breaking the hull open, casting the men ashore, and leaving Rico to fight for his life in the rugged surf.

With a small lull in the battering waves, Rico hangs on to a piece of the hull and keeps his head up. He wonders how Alex fared in the crash and keeps a squinty eye out for his shipmate, but the current tugs him South away from the wreckage. With legs growing numb, he recalls those daily trips to the vineyard to work on Don Hilario's estate, harvesting grapes and carrying the wooden jugs full of acerbic Spanish grog. To Rico, it was all vinegar, but his father swam in it. His father would repeat every morning,

"Rico, my son, remember to bring me a globe of wine."

"Si, padre, por seguro."

Fearing the threat from his father, Rico would lament day after day. He would walk along the warmer Atlantic shore dreading another long day, picking, and packing at the estate. Sometimes he would walk along the black mossy rocks, jumping from jagged rock to rock, and other times on the smooth sand. Once, he picked up a greenish-black mussel shell, grotesquely mossed over on one side, but when he turned it over, it radiated a hologram of rainbow colors that made him hopeful. He held the shell up to the light in front of the horizon and heard:

The color of me is in the sea...

Wonderful music reverberated with the beat of the waves, crashing, and rolling on his feet. The sound of his father's voice would drown out. To his left, mussels aggregated on the rocks with a desperate swinishness for space. On his right, however, a symphony of discovery called him, where he escaped into possibilities beyond his 12 year-old mind. He heard more hypnotic chants:

when you don't watch me
I send ground swells your way
pulsing my waves
like a young heartbeat
timed to pounce on your shores
a steel pulse beating the earth's drum
to the rhythm of the tides
undulating in northern and southern hemispheres

Wave by wave, lyrics from afar would roll in. Barrel after barrel of the sound would break as they crashed on the shore.

when I don't hear from you
I crash onto your jagged, rocky reefs
rattling your beaches like mini quakes
howling winds and whipping sand
into your ears
sticking to your wax
engraining your soul
when you don't taste me
I concentrate my tears
salting the sea more
parching your tongue
with a bubbly stew of sea
when you don't touch me
I spring forth my living waters
and shine forth God's light
through fanned-out pinwheel waves
unraveling my spirit

stored up in the deep
and when you don't sail my seas
I always show you what you are missing

Still, adrift, the numbness creeps up to his waist. He kicks hard to avoid hypothermia. He scans the shore in search of sand but sees no gold on the shore, only whitewash hitting the rocks. As swift as the currents changes directions, he drifts back into his past again, this time, on a fateful day that changed the course of his life. One day when he arrived to work a few minutes early, he ran into Alex waiting for the gates of the estate to open for the day. Alex is waiting mischievously.

"Rico, I've been waiting for you. I found a few barrels of wine stored around the back of the barn that were left out of the stables. Why don't we take one of these to your father once a month instead of you swindling a jug a day? There have to be 20-30 jugs in a barrel..."

Rico laughs. "Eres loco. How will we do that, dumb burro?"

"No problem, we can run-roll it down the beach! It'll be fun," Alex exclaims.

He continues, "We can bail out of Church early on Sunday while the landlords are in mass and come back here and ride a barrel to your house and hide it in your backyard."

The boys' hometown Galicia is the burial place of Saint James the Greater and is a holy place where all must attend Sunday mass unless they are sick or invalids, so the boys must attend church with their parents. They ask their parents if they can pass Bibles out to the invalids in the town who can't attend Church. Impressed with their boy's community servitude, the parents agree. So, the boys run over to the back of the stable and find the dusty wine barrels leftover in the back.

"Rico, let's tip this barrel over and roll it down to the beach. Then, we can run on it to your house." Alex bravely suggests.

"Let's do it. If we roll it on the sand, it will have some cushion for the journey." Rico adds.

"Come here, Rico. Push up on this corner." The boys both take a deep breath and push up under the iron metal rim. The barrel shifts slightly but doesn't teeter over.

Rico springs into action and finds a hoe in the stable.

"Let's lay the hoe in front of the barrel, wedge the barrel in the dirt, and push it over the hoe from the top." The boys push, pull and push harder. After ten seconds or so, the barrel creaks and tips over, hitting the ground hard and making a small cracking sound like wood splitting, but stays intact somehow. They roll it down the hill and into the sand.

Alex jumps on the barrel like a *Jinete de Toros* and balances slowly, stepping forward, rolling it along, and shuffling slowly. He falls off into the sand and gets up again. After a few attempts, he seems to get the hang of it.

"Rico, get up here and try barrel-running. "Eres un Jinte de Toro." Once again, Rico obliges his friend as he does his kin. "Okay, hold it still for a while until I get the hang of it"

He jumps up and slightly bends his knees, curling his toes over the rusty rail and taking slow steps backward, propelling the creaky barrel forward a few feet.

"You're a natural." Alex encourages. Rico picks up the pace and rolls off the balls of his feet smoothly like a

Flamenco dancer gracing the floor in reverse. Rico breathes in the salty air and hears:

The color of me is in the sea

"Estas bailando...you are dancing, my friend." Alex rejoices. Rico keeps rolling along. He shuffles to the sound of the set waves reverberating across the beach.

Escaping the confines of the Church, they freely barrel-roll, surfing the Spanish sand and undulating the dunes foot by foot toward Rico's house until he loses his balance and rolls over the front of the barrel, slamming his right cheek into the warm unforgiving sand.

Smacked by a cold Pacific wave, Rico comes out of his memory of that day as a youngster gallivanting freely. With his right cheek stinging with brutal cold, he realizes he was knocked off his floating piece of hull. The oak wood from the hull reminds him of the same wood from the barrel he stole with Alex. He finally stops drifting and anchors himself on a thick bed of golden-brown kelp outside a brilliant cove illuminating a radiant green. With little feeling in his hands and a heavy head, he strains to locate sand on the beach, scanning with blurry vision, a safe place to beach himself. He keeps his narrow sight focused on the small cove and drifts in and out of consciousness as he floats closer and closer to shore. The ocean currents finally release him up onto the sand. With some relief, he lifts his head, rests it against the sand, and slips into unconsciousness.

Elusively, a young native woman with bright white feathers, cascading her long brown hair, scales down the cliffside. She has five wolves beside her- two ahead of her, two behind her, and one right next to her as they guide her down the treacherous mountainside. The mystical girl hypnotically weaves her wolf catcher side to side, calling the wild beasts to come to her. She dances as they weave through her chant. She raises her spear to the ocean calling out to the hawk soaring over them as if speaking to the red raptor without words. The large bird swoops lower and circles directly over the seaman's head and returns to the cliff tops.

The mysterious woman sees Rico, a curious seafarer with short, treacherous, and salt-crusted blond hair. She wonders if he is a pirate like the other swashbucklers, she has seen sail by her enchanted cove. She doesn't know about his history of the derailment, working with the conquistadors in search of El Dorado. He had been sailing with the Spanish vessels since he opted out of a jail sentence for stealing barrels of wine from Don Hilario's vineyard. - *Yes, the boys got caught that day when they stole the barrel from their employer's estate and gallivanted freely while supposedly handing out Bibles.* The estate overseer saw the boys steal the barrel and head for the beach. He chased them down, captured them, and chained them to the fence until the Don returned from Church. A theft was punishable by serving jail time for adults and work service for juveniles. Because of Don's status as a high official in the monarchy, he assigned the boys a job on a Spanish fleet *El Buscador* to recover stolen loot taken from Spain as their payback to the lord. Rico felt obligated to pay his boss, but he also wondered what it would be like to man his ship.

The native sees the soggy castaway asleep on the shore and commands the wolves to go sit along the base of the rocky cliff where she descended the trail.

'I have nothing for protection, not even my cutlass,' Rico thought. He sighs with relief when he notices the wolves retreating to the cliffside. She walks closer to him. She appears to float with the wind, emitting golden rays of sunshine through black strands of hair. Behind her, giant boulders on the cliff-side, radiate a green hue, illuminating the cove. Rico climbs to his knees. The woman steps forward. Small grains of jade glow from her toes. Rico's eyes skim upward, circumventing her tan calves and escalating higher up to her smooth inner thighs when she abruptly stops him with her spear. Alarmed, he stops gazing, stands up and takes a few steps backward. Her eyes blaze a million golden-green sunsets he's seen reflect off the glassy horizon. She says nothing, but he succumbs to her beauty and hears:

I bite my lip to hold back words
all I need is here
our gestures calm the stirring ocean
ghosts behind our heads speak as friends
reunited from a lost voyage in a disillusioned sea
muttering syllables ramble in
fragmented phrases
muffling the language within
music plays while static scratches the surface
capture, clench, and hold this melody
I listen desperately

She sticks her spear in the wet sand and folds her hands around his, blowing warm breath on his frozen hands. Her touch warms him, opening the valves to the chambers in his heart. He begins to feel on course. He is curious if she is some brave native's wife, or even worse, a chief's daughter. *I wouldn't want to be caught with a chief's daughter. He would surely take my scalp,* Rico thinks. Her beaming smile continues to warm him even more. He feels thick sand grains on the tips of his toes, and some in his heels. He takes a step closer to the woman when suddenly the alpha wolf at the base of the cliff growls and kicks aggressively with his paws on the gray-green mountain gravel. The wolf snarls at Rico but the native woman raises her dream catcher. "Sonoco" to the wolf and he silences. Rico is impressed with her command of nature.

The woman cups her hand, and charades the motion of drinking water, and points to the cliff at the end of the cove, and motions for him to follow her. She guides him to the spring. He follows and gets back some warmth in his feet. Rico drinks for a few minutes, quenching his thirst. Still delirious, he can barely stand, so he sits back against a large serpentine rock with support for his back. The squaw squeezes her fingers together, lifting them to her mouth in an eating fashion, and points to Rico, asking if he's hungry. He nods. She firmly motions for him to wait, walks back to the wolves, and hikes up the trail with the pack.

While the woman is gone Rico dozes off to sleep for several minutes and wakes to a tingle on the surface of his arms and legs. With his hands and feet finally thawed out, he stands and explores the beach. He twists his feet side to side in the dry black sand. A wave crashes on the shoreline and rolls up the slope to his feet. When the water hits the sand, it turns from black to a sparkly jade green like the woman's toes. He studies the cracks and crevices of the mountainside and realizes there are huge chunks of dark-green rock falling from the cliff onto the beach and turning into translucent sand. This must be the jade that Alex used to talk about on their journeys to China in route to trade spices and gold.

If only Alex knew about this, Rico muses. *He had always carried on about how the women were different here and how the color of the minerals was brilliant. He loved the earthy minerals more than gold because they were surprises along the way and not a means to an end.* But Alex would do anything to get his hands on this jade.

Rico wonders when the woman will return. He glances up the trail to the edge of the cliff but sees no one. He keeps searching the cove and comes across a shell that looks like a large clam with the curved side facing up. He picks it up, turns it over, and an array of rainbow colors levitate from the abalone shell, and he hears:

No matter how far you travel over land and through the sea, the truth is you are near me

Rico wonders if he is still sleeping. He grips the shell tighter, slicing his index finger on a worn-out sharp edge of the abalone shell. Blood drips from his finger. He picks some cruciferous plants from the cliffside and rubs soothing plant jelly on his finger, which stop the bleeding. A few minutes later, the Native woman reappears with the alpha wolf. She glides down the stairs with a bundle of venison and blackberries in her hand. Rico hears the same melody again. He eats until he is full. While regaining his strength, he marvels at her beauty. Her eyes poise perfectly like emeralds on an obsidian ocean of black shiny hair. Momentarily, he forgets that he is a young Spanish conquistador, a castaway from his ship and lost in old Mexico. He extends his right hand out gently grasping her left hand, but he feels pressure on his finger where he sliced it on the shell, which she doesn't notice. The alpha wolf growls and trots closer to her but she commands him to stop.

"Toe nook, Ha," she says, and the wolf retreats and sits.

Rico grasps the abalone shell and pulls it close to his heart and then gestures to give it to the woman. The Native woman smirks and nods her head side to side in a "no"fashion. She walks on the sand, pacing around for a couple of minutes, finds a black jagged rock with sharp edges and holds it up to Rico's heart in a charade with a question, pointing to his chest, "Your heart?"

"No," he says, but must demonstrate to the Native of another tongue. He wonders, *she must think I'm a pirate.* He finds a stick on the beach and slowly sketches out a female figure in the sand. The figure has a necklace, a feathered headdress in her hair, and a sketch of a wolf next to her. She resembles the Native woman. The Native woman smiles, indicating she recognizes that he is referring to herself. She reciprocates with a drawing of a man with wide shoulders, hoop earrings, and a sword sheathed in a swashbuckler's attire.

Feeling misunderstood, he scratches out the sword, swashbuckler, and hoop earrings. Then he takes his stick, sketches a big heart in the middle of the male figure, and points to his heart. While he is on his knees in the sand, the Native woman slides over to him. Her soft illustrious hair blankets him with warmth and bliss. She reaches out to hug him when suddenly he is jolted out of his sleep.

"Rico, we found you! We have been searching for the beaches all day for you. I am so happy we found you." Rico's eyes droop, and disappointment overcomes him. "No!" he screams back to Alex. "No, where is she? I was just with her. She was reaching out to hug and kiss me." Rico scans the sand next to him where he drew the sketch of his heart but sees no sketches or drawings anywhere on the beach. He sees no wolf paw prints nor elusive Native female footprints. There is no sign of his beautiful squaw anywhere. She has vanished as quickly as Alex startled him out of his sleep.

"Where am I?" Rico asks. "We were cast ashore two miles north, and you must have drifted overnight and into the morning and landed here on this brilliant cove," Alex explains. "And look, you have a bump on the right side of your head. You must have hit your head in the wreck! I am glad you are fine now, or are you?" Alex jokes.

"I want to go back to sleep, she was so beautiful!"

"Come back." Rico pleads.

"You are lucky to be alive, mi amigo," Alex reassures.

"But I saw one of those women you always talk about, Alex."

"Ah, you must have dreamt of a seer, or a mermaid," Alex continues.

"No, she was a Native woman with white feathers and wolves and green eyes, just like the color of the sand and the rocks on the cliffside." Rico describes.

Alex looks around at the sand, the rocks, and the cliffs, realizing where Rico got beached. "You hit El Dorado verde, mi amigo!" This whole beach is full of North American jade. Rico gets up and smiles and laughs, "Of course, mi amigo!"

The boys fill their bags with chunks and chunks of brilliant green jade and head back out to the dingy boat waiting for them to return to the recovery ship and head back home. As they are getting into the boat Rico hears:

Although it may seem I have gone away
And left my soggy castaway
Gaze into the radiant rocks of green

And sing along so blissfully
About stories of getting stranded ashore
And being saved by her Native in a land of lore

OF SONG & STITCHES

The Carrot Dangler

We desire to collaborate
Its policy corporates
We are obligated to earn
Its tendency is to spurn

It dangles carrots of many colors
until the donkey treads the ground
Sufficiently and Excessively
Meeting forecasts in the sky
Near the silver clouds
Evaporating spontaneously
As if painting a show for the gods on Wall Street
To please *their* splendor drafted
In the game of hopeful gains

And lost forecasts
Where the blame falls on
the worker digging
in the ground
seeking saturated soil
for the man in the tower
peering down on
the lesser steed,
sniffing and snorting
sensing years and years of petrified
zooplankton
enriched in black goo and refined energy
an enhanced maple syrup
for our hotcakes
steaming on the table of ours and our kin,
and kinship that leads to kind-ship
and in Hawaiian-a KineShip

A play unlike the natural tides of the earth and moon
Where surfers glide the surface
And dance on waves
Of mother nature's gifts
Bestowed to us
Gravity in a box
Unraveled and Opened up for us
To enjoy
A present from the Maker

We rely on the farmer
And his crafty hand
To nurture the ground
Let water flow
And sunlight bless
Nature's bounty
And harvest the crop
For us all

They rewrite the rules
As to balance the scale of production
To skim the cream from the crop
And bury the rewards
Often enticed by
The Officers will...

Under him, EGO grows

Expected Gains
Greater Goals
Over-Reach

We strive to partner in groups
To obtain our goals
For our own incentive and that of
The larger group-the community

They conspire to own the partner
The group and the goal
And to feed the ass
That chases
The carrot of various colors

When we work, we go to gather
carrots for the pot
To cook with butter and brown sugar
for the relish of our family
a strong sense of identity

One must ask,

Am I *Dangler*?
Am I Farmer?
Am I Worker?

Shall we sow these seeds of toil?

When you get beat down and tired,
Stop and observe nature
I urge you to watch Dragonflies mate
For when they join
Their shape is inevitable
Invincible
And most victorious

Our First Song

At first, we are cast out
into the wild sea
Hopeful that mom and dad won't flee
But choose to attach us to their boats
That float and drift and drag along
Searching for land

Once ashore, we anchor in sand to mature and
yearn our shadow's purpose
In the garden's light
we stand
barefoot, where we toil
Scraping the sacred ground

Stuck by thorns
We mettle with nettle
Numbing the pain
We must endure
Until harvest time

Respire

Collaborate with me
As a whole body
Like a green organism breathing
Respiring...
Integrated with a cerebral halo
Reverberating above and around
Approaching homeostasis
Our branches reach out with
Stems and leaves that relay info
From one cell to the next

Where our ciliated leaves expire oxygen
Our nose inhales a mystical vapor
Our sporous chin protrudes
Breathing in and out
Sipping bubbles from carbonated suds
That pop and float above the soil

We must chlorophyll our whole brain
With a light transformation
Into glucose
A sugary delight
That signals every leaf on every branch to open up
And capture vibrational light
Converting more energy into inspiring the whole tree

A sweet sap for the bark, branches, and phloem
Layers of chloroplasts
Stack a pigmented bunch of sponges
Absorbing rays attenuated to serene green

The halo of waves bouncing off our cerebral screen
Resonate an invisible aura that our eyes can't see
But our sense of healing can overcome
When we respire as a whole
Our vitals infuse us with life sustaining
Elixir that drugs alone cannot provide

Approaching balance, we
Function as one, supporting every leaf on our tree
Fueling life, perpetuating wonder and pleasure
At a constant pace toward healing

Swish & Soup

At home:

On the corner of Noriega &
The Great Highway, the younger brother plays,
stuck in the shadow
of his big brother, Aaron, a basketball star.

So, he takes to gaming-day and night,
setting up in the basement below,
putting on his own virtual gaming show.

He is surrounded by a shroud of fog
Condensed from a sea of an ill society...

Hovering in a haze-his face reflects flat purple-
off the screen's bright display.

Little brother punches the keyboard
click, clack, dat-ta, tat
Da, da, click, clack, dat-ta, tat...
shooting to score points of mundane matter
raining back down on his empty platter.

But the points he scores are fuzzy
while the numbers are high, they read 33,126
Pixels fade, then radiate; fade, then radiate glow

Icons flip on
screens that snicker as light bulbs flicker.

He jerks the joystick left,
right, and straight.

He keeps on it-right, left, straight,
the score calculates...

Pixies play above pixels
Icons tower over top scores
Emojis smile, frown, and surprise
They groan, distort, retort in bright display
They dance on the screen, *well, not really dance*
But shift and blink and flash over and over again

On the court:

playing for the *Dons*, Aaron shoots, *Swish*, and scores!
Shoot, *swish*, and scores again-making points count!
Dons: 36, Spartans: 21
Rumbles reverberate from the roar of the crowd
Society cheers, jumping up and down
Wooden floorboards rattle, announcing to the city *by
the bay*
a small civil-celebratory quake
is in play-escalating Aaron's status to *lord of the Dons*

While-

Back at home, his little brother nibbles on Cheese Nips
Sitting safe and sound
Tapping the keys underground, twisting &
Clawing to tame the virtual beast
That bestows him by day and into the night

Little brother reaches for the joystick-
but where is the joy?
Big brother shoots and scores some more...

Lost, he:

He swims in a social soup-

A whirlpool
Surrounds him...
Sending him friend requests
Warm and fuzzy, in theory.

He dips his toes in
From time to time
Swirling his feet in the psylicon-sand
Info-bytes bubble up
Unscrambling the code of the ocean

Virtually-

Rocking the mainframe
Causing tech-tonic shifts
Sending tsunamis across cyber continents
Where societal storms blow across the surface, squalling
Wind waves of wonder

A cauldron of opinion travels swiftly
Comment to comment
From the rebound of the second information age
From the forest of the mainframe
Toward the tides of tyranny
Into the spam of software worn scandals
Eroding into pixie hard drive dust

Where gold assets are left behind
And Bitcoins pave the way
The glitter of silver and bits of gold construct its interior

But lose its value in the digital madness
Of zeros and ones
Where transmission sizzles hot...

Then Evaporates
To form precipitous clouds
Storing bytes and bytes
Of vapor
Raining back down on the
Mad Hatters that catch the crazies
On their platters

Will he be ready for the wave?
Will it lift him up and throw him on his back?

Marking his individuality with a number
Branding his digital religion
Pinning him to a concrete metric-an infinite algorithm
that never ends-like pi
An eternally repeating decimal,
Jack's beanstalk in the sky

He will keep his wit-coins about him:
Personal, health, and financial
He won't let it be his whim, but yours!

He cherishes his magic beans
So they may sprout in his sandy garden
With ice plants and beads of dew
Settling on salty ridden air-searching for
Real soil and weeds that climb to his porchlight

He centers his CPU
Where its servers cook up big ideas

And spit them out like taffy

Chewable
Undeniable
Exposed

Will he have chips or wafers for lunch?

We urge him to drop the joystick
And take up surfing
Along the wispy shores and sandy dunes

He waxes up his board
With his viral shield and rides it out
Into the frozen ice cream headache waves
Salty and swirly, sand saturates his hair
As he gets thrown onto the shore and into the dry sand

With numb fingers and an icicle nose, he realizes
He is not cut out for surfing waves in the ocean

So, he returns to his basement
To thaw out from the cold and escape
An unforgiving Pacific shore
Over OB's dunes he shuffles home

He returns to drink that familiar grog
With crunch wafers
And blue-green ribbon-strip jerky
He takes a sip of the that-oh, so familiar *techno soup-*
Feeling right at home.

KineShip

KineShip is
Hawaiian kine
Cali kine
isle Man
mainland
Wahine
bikini

a shakka sign
a unique design
two hands shaking
ship to ship

one of many cold sails
another curved and designed
for warm waves

above Mano
below Akua
with the wind
a mind bridge
sky surfing
a flat rainbow
C & H style
California beets
island cane sugar
sprinkled
on my cereal

Volkswagens & rusty Toyotas
road trips around the island
up and down the poppy coast

a golden blanket warming
mother nature's bright bed spread

awaken our senses in spring time
waterfalls carve ridges into your
jagged volcanic mountains like
grooves in a giant chocolate Hershey's kiss
with ridges flaking off we watch them dig
back down to Pele's inferno
in the oven of the Pacific
a giant cauldron of coco
magma and lava
bubbling up forming
new earth every day
in nature's unstable
belly-button
where Kilauea
flows to the ocean

to chill Cali-style on the
Big Sur coast in a field of wildflowers
or to talk story wit da braddah's
at Pinetrees

watching the waves
roll along the beach
telling da kine and da
other kine
hello, Hibiscus,
all pau Poppy
Until next time Mahalo!

Mauna Kea

on her navel's peak
they turn the lens around to
keep the Aloha

TAKE PAUSE, AMERICA

Personal essay written during COVID shutdown,
Sept. 2020

The days of normality are gone forever but not forgotten. We are entering a new frontier-a time where we must step off our treadmills and engage with our kin. We are faced with an opportunity outbreak but are we courageous enough to take that leap of faith? Are we open to reconsidering connecting with our kids, grandparents, and lost friends? I invite you to play in this paradoxical moment in time where it takes a flu-like virus and global anxiety to move us out of normal and into the extraordinary. Here is your chance to resolve that dispute with your family member, ask your boss for a promotion, create an addiction recovery plan, or dive into that thesis brewing in your imagination.

There couldn't be a better time in history than now to unseat the ill-crowned in the political arena, the social arena, and the obvious biological domain. *First, we must all take a moment of mindfulness to pray for those afflicted by the coronavirus and support them medically and emotionally.* We hope those in quarantine find peace, comfort, and re-engagement with their friends and family. The stray biological mRNA we call COVID-19 has cleverly found its way into our genome and is mutating a rapid rate. But, despite, its athletic performance of jumping from the animal organism to the human body, we can still uncrown the powerful plasmid with strategic social positioning and sharp aseptic technique. It wants us to haphazardly connect-person to person until it has corrupted all of humankind. We have ironically come together, virtually, to stop it biologically. Musicians are playing songs at home, educators are learning to teach online, and employers are allowing many people to work at home.

Socially, we must find the courage to trust our community leaders and collaborate with educators and employers to facilitate healing. Finding strength deep down inside is also paramount. How do we manage our anxiety and concerns? In my five years living in this Silicon Valley suburb, I haven't seen so many families taking walks together, riding bikes, and laughing along with the uncomfortable situation we are in. Can they figure out a way to enjoy each other without neurotically checking their phones to appease their bosses or ill-fated fancies? I think so. *This is the global reset we all need.* A giant social refresh will slow us down and force us to focus on our priceless families and their individual needs. It makes you wonder why we couldn't have otherwise found a way to prioritize our friends and families first?

Some positive side effects of the COVID-19 pandemic:

- This is your jubilee moment-a time to rest and reset for the balance of forgiving debts and refreshing financial plans
- With this new paucity, begin a new senior thesis or finishing your doctoral one
- Overcome racist feelings with the expansion of love and acceptance-releasing discomfort and the shackles of uncertainty
- My brother in law's rotating schedule has allowed him to be home half the week and teach his 3-year-old son to ride his bike. He was able to remove the training wheels this week vs. a projected six months from now
- Family reuniting daily taking walks, playing games, doing home-projects, making love, helping children with homework, etc.
- Graduates struggling to pay student loan debt may get a temporary breather
- Create something non-productive to society but fulfill a personal goal like sculpting or painting
- Rest and rejuvenation
- Start the home renovation project you couldn't get to
- Evaluate how your boss treats you. Are you truly happy there? Explore other healthier opportunities. Network, reconnect virtually
- Prune the dead leaves and branches from your life
- Exercise in your house or neighborhood

- Plant a garden in the yard as a family event
- Struggling business find new strategies and opportunities to adapt
- For young investors or those reticent to invest, this is an opportune time to get into the market or refinance a loan at a lower interest rate to save money. How about financial education? After all, wouldn't that benefit most of those in the middle class and lower socioeconomic groups?
- Struggling couples can work on communication and problem solving
- Global change in the management of animals and the environment
- Boost healthcare quality, supplies, and practitioner safety
- Get an advanced degree and return to school
- People are giving each other space in lines at the ATM, in lines at Peets coffee, and large crowds in general
- Cleanse the country and world of corruption. Examples are the college admissions scandal and recent Senate members sell-off from inside information, and cleaning up "wet animal markets"

In the wake of the coronavirus pandemic, what is your opportunity?

Well, I wrote a brief paper on my personal beliefs last fall in 2019 for one of my graduate-level classes in clinical psychology at Pepperdine University. Unaware of what 2020 would bring, I explained in my essay what I thought was plaguing America of its time and creativity. And now, with hindsight, I see a way to help our community with my education, experience, and talents. Interestingly, this viral outbreak has created an opportunity for me to spring into action and utilize my personal beliefs and values today at an accelerated pace. See the bulk of my essay below from a class on the *Theories and Principles in Family Counseling,* written in Sept. of 2019 before the outbreak.

~Excerpt~

Now, more than ever, we have so many demands on us to perform in society as money-making contributors and law-abiding citizens. How are we to keep up with these demands but also find joy and happiness? Because it is so expensive to survive, we must work two or three jobs to pay the rent and bills. It should be no surprise to anyone in this community that this leaves very little time for developing familial and personal relationships. We are pushed to perform like green springs spitting out tons of money to pay everyone around us and hopefully ourselves sometimes. The world of psychology is all about relationships good and bad, positive and negative, and healthy and unhealthy. I find it fascinating that the stress and pressure of performing in this expensive society are where a huge amount of our distress comes from. We should be spending a whole lot of time with our children, but we are at work 8-10 hours per day and too tired to play with them when we get home because we must sleep to recover. Children don't understand the demand we face to survive in this material world. Lovers may understand it, but they don't like it. Many of us are struggling to find joy but we only get glimmers of hope because of this unrighteous beating of the money drum to make it and keep it.

I am motivated to help members of my community, state, and even nation find the courage to make decisions that make them happy and find joy. I am up for the challenge of facilitating ideas, creative plans, and even disrupting the status quo. I would love to help us all get out of this ugly carrot and donkey game that robs us of our valuable time with our friends and family. I am confident that I can help empower individuals in families to find the courage to creatively carve a joyful life out of this confusing place. *If I can empower individuals, then they can, in turn, empower their family members and so on to play a rewarding game of finding joy in their work lives and family lives.*

What qualities do I have to contribute to resolving this problem? Because I found a way to strike a work-life balance for fifteen years, I feel I can help other members of my community do the same. For example, during my first two years in corporate America, I commuted one to two hours per day and sat in a cube for 6-8 hours per day and then would come home exhausted with very little energy for my wife. I began to realize I had to find more time for my own life as I was on a slow treadmill to misery and death. I had to find the courage to ask my boss for a day working at home or one day off in the middle of the week. The opportunity struck when I had orthopedic surgery and had to rehabilitate 3 times a week. I got a doctor's note to go to physical therapy 3 days a week for 3 months. I realized I felt so much better when I had three days at home telecommuting and two days at work all day busting out production.

At this point, a shift occurred in my life I learned the art of designing my own life and not allowing any managers to enslave me at work. I began incorporating this newfound creativity into my family life, fitness life, and even personal life for hobbies. After successfully doing this for a decade or so I realized I must share my newfound freedom with others. The breakthrough was in finding the courage to communicate effectively with my boss at work by taking risks that allowed me to be at home with my family more. I wrote up proposals for raises and when I performed well, I would ask for days off or regular telecommuting days at home where I had more flexibility when appropriate. These are examples of some of the challenges I will help my clients to find freedom in their lives. Freeing up creative space will help them tackle their emotional issues.

I found myself talking with co-workers more and more about work-life balance and courage. I realized a few employees dared to challenge themselves and their bosses at allowing them to telecommute if they could in their jobs. My new mission at work became to advocate in secret to help others find happiness in their daily lives. I was overjoyed that I could motivate others to attempt these challenges and achieve them. Every couple of months or so my secret alliance with my coworkers would pay off when they would share success stories with me about how they got one or two days approved to work at home. I felt a lot of satisfaction in their successes and longed to do this more. Other times, co-workers would confide in me with stories about their spouses or significant others and I would carefully offer up creative ideas like writing letters to spouses when stuck or strategizing on ways to open communication. I loved it and developed a passion for helping others. This leads me to where I am today in pursuing my Masters in Marriage and Family Therapy.

How do I think people change? People change when they are in unbearable pain-emotionally and physically. Pain is our indicator that we need to make changes in our lives. The leverage we have as therapists is to recognize that pain and springboard off it with creative ways to alleviate it and resolve the underlying problem. Of course, our goal is to empower the client so they can manage their own lives efficiently and effectively. But, effectively meeting the client in the "here and now" is essential. I resonate with humanistic and existential approaches as well as CBT when more structure is needed. I am open to learning an integrated approach naturally as I develop the skills in practicum under great supervision. When our clients begin to trust us and develop an alliance, change happens! Relationships are the vehicle of change and I believe in treating our clients with human decency and unconditional love. I am aware at times that it will be challenging to embrace certain problems and personal matters but am open to getting my counselor to discuss transference issues that may affect my practice.

What settings and populations do I want to serve? For me, it is difficult to say I want to focus only on one area of my community or client population because everyone human is affected by family and friends and how they communicate. I can't imagine turning away anyone who is struggling to find a way to solve a psychological problem where I believe I can help. Because I have been married, divorced, and remarried with two children, most of my experience is from the perspective of a husband and father who loves his family and makes them the priority in life. I have endured and resolved many familial issues for the last 18 years, so I am comfortable in the family therapy setting. Besides, I have battled two different forms of arthritis and managed the pain and discomfort that accompanies chronic conditions like Rheumatoid and Osteoarthritis. I will also specialize in counseling those with chronic pain. I have utilized an integrated approach to managing my chronic pain and plan on doing so for my clients.

~End of excerpt~

To sum up, when I wrote this essay, I was mainly focused on helping my local community but now in the wake of this viral outbreak, I realize we all can make global change. What America needs is a giant social therapy session where emotional intelligence and love are in the driver seat. While police reform and other external sources may help enforce laws to regulate group behavior, the real change comes from within individuals.

Because racism is related to hate which is related to one's view of oneself. To change anything that requires emotional intelligence, the concept of self-perception must be changed in the first order, then second-order change may happen for the future (clubs, groups, schools, churches), then higher on up-ideally third-order change (communities and societies). *Enforcing rules on people externally does not permanently change from within because it is fear-based and temporary.* But change from within internally amplifies in magnitudes that will help heal. One must understand hate which is the opposite of love before any movement can happen with racism. A positive approach would be to empower individuals, families, and groups to love from a moral standpoint. This moment in time is a window of opportunity to explore the motivation in change and stretch our perceptions of ourselves and how we should interact with our neighbors.

As a society, we are failing the emotional intelligence test currently and must fight hate with love. America needs an emotional and educational reform where love is in the driver seat. Any ideas? What are some love-based philosophies, teachings, and practices? Perhaps an idea may be to replace one working day per week with *friends and family day* to build our emotional intelligence and create more space and time for each other. This could do wonders for our lack of understanding of each other. Less overintellectualizing and more collaboration may be what the doctor ordered. Let us, America, find the time and motivation to propose one change for us all so we may prosper once again.

What is your specialty and how will you contribute to third-order change? However, when this viral tsunami subsides, will you be ready for a global change and universal transformation?

MAIZE OF COLOR

During the time of the ancient world in this land, the color was a gift of light granted to us to determine the vitality of plants, animals, and the weather. What our eyes would not see our ears would hear by listening to sound and our skin would feel the radiant heat of the sun:

Is there glistening yellow, blues, reds, and shiny black inside the green fibrous husk?

Can you hear the wrestle of the wind against the grass?

Can you feel the chill of the breath from the north?

When does the warm blanket lie upon us from the south?

In the first world, natives of this land would strip back layer upon layer of thick green husk until-

They discovered the kernels that appeared to float with an iridescence of earthy red and terracotta matte, a brilliant blue like the edge of their earth near the sea, warm browns like the dirt under their feet, and a shiny black like their daughter's long lustrous hair.

As hundreds and hundreds of years passed and even thousands, the lighter people from across the sea to the east came ashore. They brought beans and grasses, and fat pigs, and a large yellow kernel that grew bigger than any native maize of its time. For another hundred years or so they grew more and more of this hefty yellow corn in rows and rows until no iridescence was found in a stripped shuck of corn.

Along with them, they brought strong black men and women with wild hair and dried figs to eat on the ships that sailed to our land. The figs they carried had skins thicker than ours and enduring like the oak trees on our plains. They made the black men and women work the rows of maize and other stems, stalks, and vines until they fell to the ground only to get back up again-day in and day out. Meanwhile, the corn got bigger and yellower until it filled the belly of our land. Pigs got bigger and the white man got fatter.

After some time, a big war broke out where the white and black men were fighting each other with hissing and snapping machines that sounded like the pop in a wildfire. They fought for several years until the black man stopped working in the fields of yellow corn. Meanwhile, we had a harder time finding land to live on and hunt on as the white man pushed us away from our heartland. We settled to the north where the breath was colder and on the edges of the earth where we found shellfish and salmon.

For some time after the black man left the fields, we heard that the yellow corn began to rot and smell like a dirty swamp with no running rain. During the springtime, we left one of our terracotta brave men behind with the white man because he hurt his leg and could not sit on a horse. He lived with the farmer and saw the problem of rot and loss of yield to the corn. He remembered a medicine man who told him, "When the color of kernels turns all white, our people will die."

That night he had a vision of his ancestors holding up a human-sized ear of maize with the most illustrious colors emanating from the husk. The tribal leaders danced around a fire passing the huge ear of corn from one member to the next, each one taking a different color kernel and roasting it on the fire. They had a large feast-feeding on the multicolored maize that fed their nations.

The next day, the lame native woke from his powerful dream and had the white farmer take him to the base of the mountains where a few multicolored plants remained. He searched for seeds that spoke of his ancestry as far back as the Pawnee and the Cherokee of the indigenous nations that illuminated the colors of their cloaks, spears, and skies.

He chanted, "take these stalks, pull them from the ground, and restore the maize of color by sprinkling the kernels with care among your sick yellow rows and you will heal the crop.

The white farmer heeded his advice, thanked him, and collected the seeds. The farmer built a small, wheeled chariot and attached it to his horses so the disabled native could plant them in designated rows to amplify the colors of his ancestors.

Several months later, new kernels transformed the corrupt yellow kernels into a brilliance of blue, black glass, purple hue, and deep red terracotta matte-announcing stability for the crop and acceptance of his people in the spirit of fall.

MOVES THAT MARVEL

Sitting on my floating vessel
Opposing the shore
I gaze upon a gazelle-
skipping across water swells:

Drawing up
Shaping to roll
Hollow
Glass cylinders *inside*
Feathery wonders *outside*

Mist blows on my face
From her under-the-lip-snaps
Sending telegrams of hope my way

She makes moves that marvel

A trace of her iridescent blue suit
gyrates through
a water tunnel
Her fingers caress the walls
melting the glass
with streaks of water prints
disappearing evasively behind her

She creates art on water
Expressing her easel
Effortlessly...

Painting blue and white across waves of wonder!

She makes moves that marvel

She dances on water
In search of the satin tunnel
Where times stops and echoes
Whisper through the time chamber
imprinting memories forever
Sounds to cherish
And long to recapture
As I wax up my vessel every time

Her bronze hands throw beads of spray
wispy and white
as to cast a spell on hopeless waves tumbling
to shore
unaware of the dissipation
they must suffer as
they fade into the sandy slopes
diagonal to the surface of the Pacific-near the equator-
where energy is transferred instantly
millions of times a day

But she is no witch, no curses about her
No barrel with brew
No toe without a ring

Her moves make me marvel
As she dances on water

And, just when you think she sees you,
she turns around
to catch another wave

With wings outstretched,
she captures the wind

Gliding like a
Like a sail against the *Trades*
She floats above the surface

Prancing over the lip
Like an aqueous cat
Scaling tin roofs
Slipping side-ways but
Landing on clotheslines
Capturing her feline fantasy
On a whim of a wave
Dispelling the myth that cats
Do not like water...

She carves through cream
Cutting back into the tunnel-deep behind the curtain

Eyes beaming forward, I lean in
Can you see me?
Steam from the large cavern obstructs my view

Suddenly, she appears...
Floating on a white velvet foam ball-momentarily.
She shoots out
A cannonball across the sea
Right past me!

She dances away
Making moves that marvel

OUR SOVEREIGNTY

Visitors, wolves, slyly cloaked in wooly white fur,
Claim your island in the middle of the Pacific
but seize an available one.
Our stones may lead south through the Pacific
but ask for approval, a permission of sorts, like your
neighbors do.
For your Shepard teaches,

> "The earth is the Lords and all the land and
> sea creatures abide with him."

Preserve our fragrant Plumeria for embrace
Breathe the breath of Lono and flourish from his spirit
Keep the sovereign lei of Liliuokalani sweet and fragrant

Open your eyes. Can you see Pele's gift to the earth?
Her belly button undone, feeding
our archipelago for days...creating timeless islands that
march to paradise, our promise land.

And, pleasing your mother nature's landmass
of North America
Pele's sister Kilauea yields fresh lava for landmasses
Forming mirages in the sea where sea farers rest
on long journeys
Recalling fantasies of lost paradise found

Again, please do not claim your power from your Shepard
for he teaches,

> "Do unto others as you would have done unto you."

Don't you see the speck in your eye
tainting your morality?
Ask your neighbor to look for you...

Find your own steppingstone and shine it so, but
be a nation of your word, honesty, and golden glow.
When the aloha spirit has struck
speak forth and grow...
Until then,
Mahalo!

OPPOSITION

It is in opposition
that I suspend between Helios and Jupiter
lying low in the solar dust kicked up by Helios
and her magnetic pulses
spat out and orbited around into a
a giant cinnamon twist.

To my back, the warmth of her slowly fades
as she drops below blankets of stardust
that cast a rosy light into the night.
A fruitful spatial delight—
As I lay back, Luna rises in white
then does her magic as she morphs
into shades of yellow and gold.
By the time she reaches the universal roof
she has transformed into a silvery strawberry
pancake that you won't see at breakfast time.

Natives from across the land gather crates
and baskets weaved with straw.
They plan for harvest in morning to pluck the red berry
that waits with morning dew and drizzly fog
beading on the green leaves of the crop.

Once a year in June she has a chance to presume,
a place in space to steal the light
from other planetary delights,
even Jupiter in all his circular might
entices her with layers of promise that Luna
can't escape...

She floats to him blushing and blooming
with a celestial desire to be the most adorned body
in the sky.

WEASEL REEF

Taylor and Johnny-Boy gaze out at the glass and sip on hot coffee as beautiful barrels roll across the reef. The two surfers in the line-up surge up, down, and over the swells that draw waves from the deep Pacific to the triangular reef naturally formed under their boards. They wax up their boards in anticipation of capturing a few of mother ocean's jade gems of joy, delivering to the coast's sneakiest of all reefs, where finicky shelves of shacks are meant to house the chosen few that can ride this place. *This is where unicorns are caught, treasure is discovered, and waves are ridden.*

After scaling the steep cliff and tiptoeing the jagged rocks, Taylor disturbs the peaceful glass with his toes and sends ripples back out to the Pacific. Johnny-Boy jumps in and paddles out first; he snags a quick little inside wave that covers him up quickly and spits him out like a cannonball from Black Beard's ship. He turns toward Taylor with eyebrows stretched, eyes rounded and shouts,

"Whoa, Nice!"

As Taylor paddles out to gain pole position, the mysterious surfer on the outside drops in deep behind the back door and *weasels* under the lip and right into a hollow green cylinder of surprise and then in three seconds surfs right out from under the curtain with ease. Taylor chooses the next wave as the previous surfer spins around and drops in, blocking him from the position in the pocket. Taylor wonders,

'Looks like he's staking his claim to this green seafoam treasure.'

Taylor flips his board over and falls onto the jagged reef under water. As he paddles back out, the sea-going miner smirks at him, demonstrating his claim on the beach and waits for another wave. Tit for tat...next time Taylor will shoulder hop the salty miner's treasure. His chance comes with the next set of waves. Like a duel in a western film, the salty dog surfer, secures the position in front of him. He takes the same one Taylor wants and twists around behind him into priority position. *Positioning yourself for priority at Weasel Reef is as challenging as fighting for the inside track at a NASCAR event.*

Taylor reaffirms his intention and drops in on the wave in front of the stranger, spraying water droplets his way and pulling into a nice head-high tube that peels toward the cliff. Taylor gyrates through the barrel and enjoys a greenhouse view of the water tunnel, watching the top close in on the roof of his view, where the spectators watch up on the cliff up above. He can see them through the jade green tube-at the end of a rolling kaleidoscope of sparkling golden reflections off the face of the wave.

The salty sea miner paddles over to Taylor with guns a blazing; iris' dilated and eyes bulging out of his sockets as if Taylor stole his gold. Barnacles of salt crystalize on his 1970s style sandy silver-blond mustache and wild waves curl from his wiry surf-style hair.

He threatens Taylor ferociously, "Take another wave of mine and I will break your stick in half!"

Taylor's adrenaline pumps as he tries to suppress any reaction of retaliation too quickly. His heart beats like a locomotive as his concept of time slows down with introspection.

The other surfer in the line-up paddles over to Taylor.

"Hey dude, you know who that is? That's Barrel Bill... and he doesn't share these waves with anyone, not even his own son!"

Taylor asks the bystander, "Oh, yeah... How did he get his name?" The surfer replies,

"Barrel Bill used to steal barrels of wine from the *Highlands Distillery* on the shore of the San Lorenzo River and run-roll 'em all the way to the river mouth where he would drink bottles of wine with his friends on the beach."

With an eyebrow of surprise Taylor inquires further,

"You mean he would run on the barrels like log rolling?"

The surfer elaborates,

"Yeah, he's the only dude that can do it, but got caught and thrown in the slammer a couple times. I wouldn't mess with him bro, he'll pound you."

Taylor acknowledges, nods, and agrees,

"He's like my dad's age but I can see his barrel rolling skills transfer nicely over to barrel riding these killer waves."

Taylor wasn't about to roll over for Barrel Bill and his intimidation. He's had several years' experience working his surfing rotation in with Hawaiians like Titus, the Irons brothers, and Laird guys. He even scraps often here with the crusty crabs here on the much colder Cruz coast. Besides, these waves are awesome and well-endowed with island-like juice.

Another three-wave set rolls in and Johnny-Boy paddles into a nice wave that propels him inside near the cliff. The bystander surfer grabs the second wave and rides it all the way to the beach. The third wave approaches and Taylor commits but Barrel Bill appears to be thinking the same thing again. He drops in at pole position, but Taylor follows through, stalling in the bottom turn for a quick second and then cuts up into the lip, ripping the top of the wave off. He looks over his left shoulder and sees Barrel Bill, eating his wake and snarling with vengeance.

Bill pulls out of the wave and sprint-paddles over to Taylor, staring and glaring at him with anger. He splashes him a few times in the face and kicks him underwater in the legs and screams, "I told you I would break your stick in half, well"... he pauses for a second and then grabs Taylor's board, then flips it over and breaks a skeg (fin) off with his hand and rips some fiberglass off in the process but slices his hand opens on the torn glass. Blood is gushing out of his hand as he looks in disbelief.

He yells more, "Let's take it to the beach!"

They paddle to shore and by this time Johnny-Boy is by Taylor's side paddling with him. After about five minutes of paddling and about two hundred feet, they walk upon the sand. Blood continues to squirt all over Taylor's board and in the sand. Bill appears stunned and pauses in disbelief,

"Let me see your board."

He keeps bleeding on Taylor's board and asks, "Where are you from and what do you think you are doing here?"

"My name is Taylor and I live at the Summit currently and grew up in Hanalei, surfing the North Shore of Kauai."

Taylor's brain lights up like lightning as instant karma is actualizing in full form. Cloud central has been keeping its *omniscient eye* on Taylor for years and demonstrates its power instantaneously. Taylor responds to Barrel Bill with,

"Why are you so bitter? You have these perfect waves to surf every day..." Bill defensively replies,

"You have a lot of nerve. Guys like you come here thinking they can surf here without respecting us. If you do this to the Choco boys, they'll pound you... Ho, the Choco boys will bar you from their unreal waves in Hawaii."

Taylor further secures his confident position with,

"I know, I got chased around by the locals for seven years on the north shore of Kauai. It's part of the Houle hazing process and I lived here for half my childhood too."

Barrel Bill pushes his point further,

"When I surfed Hanalei, they hounded me too; the Choco boys won't stand for you trying to take their waves!"

His eyes glaze with intensity... "They knocked me out of there!"

"I know brah, you have to earn their respect, show Aloha and ask permission to date their Wahines," Taylor jokes.

Bill tries to hold back his smile but laughs a little... and at this point, Taylor figures he will name drop a couple to validate his point,

"You know Chaz Johnson?"

Bill quickly replies with surprise, "Yeah, I used to work with him at the Distillery, loading wine barrels and shipping cm out. No way... I can't believe it."

Taylor jumps in, "I went to church with him for years"

Bill starts to do a one-eighty and turn his attitude around. He turns to my board and analyzes the broken skeg. The blood from his laceration continues to ooze and dries on the deck of Taylor's *Island Creations* board. It is his favorite thruster. Bill pauses with regret and apologizes,

"I am sorry I broke your skeg...I have a barrel of wine in the back of my truck, or I can give you $20 to fix your fin, if you are okay with that?"

Johnny-Boy, who was standing by the scene, jumps in and requests, "We'll take the barrel of wine." I nod and wonder how many bottles are in a barrel. Bill confirms, "I need to wrap this cut and then I will get out the barrel for you guys."

He scales back up the rocks and up the dirt trail to his truck. Johnny-Boy and Taylor chat all the way up the trail about how lucky they are to have avoided a fight and how they scored a free barrel of wine. Johnny-Boy shares,

"Tay, we scored...I think sixteen bottles come in a typical barrel, at least the ones we used to buy for the restaurant (Johnny-Boy manages an Italian restaurant). Johnny proposes,

"That's like 2-3 bottles a guy if we call everyone and have a barbecue tonight!"

The boys approach Barrel Bill and his red Toyota 4X4 with an old camper shell. He opens the back and hands a barrel of wine to Johnny and then turns to Taylor and hands him a $20 spot. As he closes the shell the guys notice 3 or 4 more barrels in the back.

He pleads, "Here's a twenty to fix your fin. And please don't say anything to Chaz if you see him again soon!"

Taylor agrees and reassures him," "No worries."

On their way home, the boys replay the story repeatedly in awe and are thankful for the positive outcome. They invite Buffalo over to enjoy some tasty lamb chops, coupled with some *Wonder Wines* from the Distillery. Buffalo knows his wines and will have to evaluate the score. They update him on the day, and he obliges to cruise over. Buffalo shows up and sits down to join them for some apricot lamb chops and vino. He opens the barrel and gazes with amazement,

"Holy Vinoli! These are bottles *of Ridgeline, 1982,* the best Merlot to come out of California or out of the world, for that matter!"

This stuff reverberates off the tongue in three dimensions and has a cherry vanilla aftertaste."

He continues on, "and it's about $65 a bottle. That's $1,040 worth of wine. What a score! "You can buy two boards with that."

The guys pop a bottle and gather around to *talk-story* and enjoy the score of a lifetime. Taylor brings the bloodstained board in to show Buffalo. Buffalo stares at the deck for a few seconds and presents a puzzling look on his face. He indicates enigmatically,

"Guys, I don't know if you see it, but his blood dried on your board in the shape of a lightning bolt! Apparently cloud central was watching over you guys. Unreal-kind!"

THE SEEDS OF EMERY

Her mother hikes along the Greenback Ridge in the Emerald Forest. She scales the trail through the black lava rocks on the top of the mountain. The jagged boulders emit a radiant green, illustrating a forest blessed with ferns, palms, and vibrant trees clothed in brilliance.

As she reaches the peak of the extinct volcanic geyser, a golden eagle squawks behind her prompting her to turn around. She twists around to see the raptor when, suddenly, she falls into the dead geyser, landing on a bed of ferns, deep in the crust of the earth. Foliage and ferns rattle spores around her, getting in her eyes, mouth, and hair. She spits them out and shakes vehemently, attempting to get them off her human body.

Surprised, she feels a sense of peace in the crust of the earth. Warmth radiates up like a mild sauna embedded with earthy roots, clay, and flexible lattice structures, forming a net-like circular ladder to the top of the hole.

She slowly climbs her way up, like a kid on a rope-netted playground; she creeps up, step by step. She breathes in the warm waves of earth from the walls of the geyser and remembers when she was a child in Iceland playing with her family in the springs. That familiar smell comforts her as she climbs out of the hole.

She crawls out of the geyser and sees no raptor in sight. 'That was wild,' she thought and heads back to the base of the mountain near her home.

Four months later she wakes up with nausea undulating through her tired body. Curious and confused, she prods and pushes on her bloated belly, searching for answers on her condition. She feels a rounded swelling on her abdomen around her navel and doesn't recall getting her regular cycle for a few months and wonders how she can possibly be pregnant without a man in her life?

'There is no way,' she worries she is gaining weight too quickly but hasn't eaten more than usual for the last few months.

But the next morning her mother awakens to kicking in her womb…she must be pregnant! Mystified, she visits the doctor to get answers. Her doctor explains that it is scientifically impossible to conceive without a male gamete but gives her the wonderful news that she has a healthy girl growing inside her.

"I have never felt so tired, useless, and nauseated,"

Her mother explains to the doctor.

The doctor replies,

"That is a great sign… that your girl is utilizing your energy and receiving all the nutrients from you, so eat well and be happy. The ultrasound's show a thriving little one you can love and be proud of!"

Five months later her mom takes a walk to get out of the house and stretch. She walks through the base of the Emerald Forest around the perimeter of the trail. She slowly shuffles into a shallow ravine full of peat moss and rainbow trees. As she begins to climb up out of the ravine, intense cramps shoot through her voluptuous body and though her belly. She falls to the ground on her back. The peat moss transforms and thickens into a soft green bed around her, protecting her from the elements. Her mother notices the golden eagle perched above her in a brilliant tree. The rainbow trees thicken their trunks and proliferate their leaves to form a natural shelter for the soon to be the mother of the forest.

Emery is born right there in the gully of the Emerald, a forest that knew she was coming and nested her and her mother for the spectacular birth. White birch and Spruce trees admire her by displaying their normal whitebark into brilliant rainbow colors. Ferns proliferate their leaves and fill the base of trees around the site to show appreciation for the *new daughter of the forest.* White arctic wolves howl, singing songs of welcome, dragonflies flutter around in blue iridescent shine, and ants scurry and burrow in anticipation of a new leader.

Emery's mother is exhausted with the birth but overjoyed at her beautiful girl and the comfort she feels from the living things around her. The rainbow trees funnel water her way through the network of branches that entangle down into the gully. As the mother nurses Emery, surrounding ferns spring off their fiddleheads, producing food for the mother to eat when hungry.

Emery thrives and grows well the first week, then her mother decides to return home with her to settle down at the base of the mountain...

At home, cozy with her mom, Emery grows up quickly playing in the security of her house and family in the rolling foothills. At age three, she hears her first creature speak to her; an ant in her backyard called out for help,

"Hey little girl, I am lost! Do you know where my colony is? I got high-jacked on the back of a lemming that was digging through our burrow and ended up here in your yard."

Emery giggled and kneeled to see what was talking to her in that high pitch voice.

"I am down here. I am the ant here on the ground."

Emery gets down on her hands and knees in the dirt and feels liquid warmth like she is melting. She curls up on her knees into a ball and chuckles at the small creature peering up at her. She views the ant through a rounded lens like a panoramic view but only focused and smaller.

The ant stands up on his hind legs and leans against her little water bubble. She naturally shrinks and shapes herself into a small water droplet to speak with the ant.

"Hang on to me!" Emery encourages.

"I will roll you over to the burrow by the fence."

"Thank you kindly, Emery, my pleasure to meet you. I am honored to meet you, let alone get a ride on your water bubble to my colony."

"Hee, hee," Emery laughs.

The lost ant thanks her and is happy to return to his nest.

As he crawls down the hole, he shares with her,

"You don't know how special you are. We are excited you finally arrived."

Emery smiles, stands back up, shaking off the water, and transforming back into her toddler self.

Close to five years pass since her experience with the lost ant when one afternoon while looking after the garden, the golden eagle circles on high above her house. Her blue eyes follow him with wonder. Fearlessly, she extends her arm out to the wild raptor. He circles once more and descends upon her arm.

"Emery, child of the Emerald, you are chosen, and it is time to hear our cry. "

The eagle continues...

"I am Grigori, the Golden. I have been watching you since you were a tiny seed."

Emery's eyes widen. "Wow, were you circling me the other day at the fiords while I was hunting for earthworms?"

Grigori nods his regal head up and down. "Always, my wonderful sprout."

Emery smiles and Grigori clears his beak and continues,

"I must share with you a serious concern. The forest has spoken. Domesticated sheep and goats have gone *mad* and chewed up many of our Birch trees, shrubbery, and ridgeline plant life."

Emery's eyebrow pinches inward with the same concern she had for the ant. She looks over her backyard ledge and curiously gazes at the ridgeline where the forest meets the valley.

"Can you take me to the ridgeline where these crazy goats have gone mad? She asks.

"Yes, I will soar and circle around the most damaged area. "

Emery hikes down the hill, following Grigori's lead, and observes the grazed foliage and crazy goats. She explores the tree and plant communities and grows concerned about the cause of this deforestation. Surprisingly, she finds stray goats climbing trees like wild cats. She draws sketches of the healthy and grazed areas and assures Grigori she will help.

"Thank you, Grigori, I will help the trees grow back their green coats."

Grigori educates Emery about the *Keepers* of the Emerald that balance out the populations of different species. He asks her,

"Do you know where the wolves are? I haven't seen them along the ridge or in the valley for some time, now."

Emery replies, "I saw one about a year ago drinking water from the lake, but none since then. "

Grigori adds,

"Without the *Keepers*, sheep and goats overpopulate and eat up all the green! Since your birth, I haven't seen many around here either."

Emery gives Grigori a birdlike nod with her neck thanking him for his wisdom,

"Thank you, Grigori, let's fly over to the enchanted side where I last saw a Keeper."

Emery *envisions* a grey and white Falcon, lifts her arms up into the air and sports beautiful grey wings with black and white feathers. Feeling light and agile, she can maneuver her way to the enchanted side of the forest. They fly over the ridgeline and swoop down into the valley beyond the edge, scanning the view. Emery indicates to Grigori,

"This is where I saw the last Keeper, drinking water near the lake. But I don't see any in sight." So, they fly further north, another hundred miles into the colder region near the Icelandic border. They land in a giant

Birch tree standing tall in the night sky. Below a pack of Keepers are gathered around the creek, lapping up silvery, moonlit water. Emery leaves Grigori in the tree and tucks her wings in descending into the bushes, *changing* into her human form. She plants her feet near the den of the Keepers, treading quietly near the flowing stream. A vigilant auntie Keeper guarding the cub's growls at Emery warning her to stay away, but Emery introduces herself,

"I am the guardian of the Emerald in the southern region and here to speak with your alpha."

The auntie Keeper replies, "His name is Fritz, and he is on the riverbank." Emery walks over to the sandy riverbank and slowly shuffles along the sand with a low humble disposition. Fritz smiles and asks, "You must be Emery, daughter of the Emerald! I have never seen a human with such a glow. My first pack spoke of you and visited your birth in the south."

Emery reciprocates, "Yes, I came to speak with you about our deforestation in the south. Domesticated goats have gone *wild* and are eating all of our foliage and shrubberies."

"Ah, the mad goats... I have taken care of a few of those in the past few years..." Fritz jokes, chuckling and snarling humorously. He adds,

"Those pathetic creatures will eat the hooves right off their own feet. Ha, ha."

Emery inquires further, "Grigori told me you can save the forest and take care of the domesticated ravaging and over-foraging?"

"Mmm, yes sweet Emery, those lazy goats make for some easy pickings and paw lickings. We used to roam in the Emerald until the caribou migrated further north up here. Your land has been too warm the last few years for the herd, and they have moved up here to colder lands."

Emery twirls her blond hair, "It has been warmer in the Emerald. I agree. Can you help us?"

Fritz smiles with charm as his fangs glisten with iridescent light. "I will see what I can do."

Fritz alerts the Keepers to prepare a journey south to Greenland,

"Keepers of the land, Emery, daughter of the forest, has come for our help! We will journey south to Greenland in search of mad goats devouring the lush green forests near the Ridgeline of the Emerald...

He continues,

Betas, follow behind me. *Gammas,* keep an eye on the cubs as we move south...

Oh, and remember to spare the turkeys for the humans near the Ridgeline...it's Thanksgiving time and we don't want domestic retaliation from the ranchers."

Emery kneels on her hands and knees and *breathes in deeply*. She stretches her neck out and shakes side to side, turning into a bright white wolf. She runs, catching up quickly to run with Fritz.

"Fritz, I am amazed at the structure of the pack. Every wolf works together harmoniously and knows their place."

"Hang out up here with me and you get to be an icebreaker, a pioneer, leading the way! Drop back with the *Betas* and you become a beacon of vigilance, and when you are feeling playful, goof-off with the *Gammas* at the tail of the pack!"

Emery inhales swiftly and exhales a wonderful puff of steam. She smoothly trots through the snow with her padded paws, cushioning her streamlined body to dance easily through the snow.

"At home with my mom, it's just us... I love it and all but running with the pack is exhilarating and fascinating. I never knew your paws where warm inside and light against the snow."

Fritz answers,

"The less you try, the more instinctual you become and blend in with nature."

Emery adds,

"I can also see around the snowy trees like I have an extra sense in my vision. I can see another mile or so...and I can smell musky trails on top of the ice!"

She curiously asks,

"The trail over here smells like cows back near the Ridgeline. It can't be from cows? Is it a Moose or something?

Fritz laughs. "It's our meat and potatoes darling. Caribou, our whole purpose for hunting, trolling, and thriving."

Just when Emery feels comfortable in the lead, Fritz's mate runs up to the apex and chimes in,

"Getting cozy up here Emery?" she barks sarcastically.

Emery replies,

"I love it, you guys are amazing. I could stay here in the pack with you forever!"

Fritz introduces Emery to Charma, his mate,

"Emery, daughter of the forest, meet my loving mate, Charma!"

Emery bows slightly and nods submissively without knowing how or why she did this. She shares with Charma,

"Thank you for allowing me to run with your leader. I am grateful."

Fritz reassures Charma,

"Emery is with us in our form for a short while; will you take her to the Betas and Gammas. *You will always be my lady.* I love you!"

Charma smiles securely. Emery is intrigued by their loyalty and bond. She wants what they have someday when the time is right...

Charma introduces her to *Watcher* Aunts and cubs of the pack. Emery learns the whole structure from Alpha to Gamma. They stop trotting south and take a break to rest with the cubs.

Emery decides to give the pack a break and stroll through the back forest on her own for a few minutes. She chases a snow rabbit into a rocky area above the resting den when to her amazement she spots a black wolf chilling on a large boulder on the bluff above her. She has seen no contrast greater than his brilliant black coat against the soft white powdery snow. She pants slowly and stops behind a big evergreen tree. She smells curious and lifts her nose up into the eerie forest air. Scents of mystery undulate down the rock, around the trees, and into her scent field. *She is mystified, a stranger from an unknown pack, all alone...*

Emery returns to the pack and settles down with the Gammas and cuddles with the cubs for the rest of their nap. They wake an hour later to Fritz howling at them, regrouping the pack. While the cubs were sleeping, he caught a plump snow rabbit and three lemmings to share with the pack. The adults share the rabbit while the cubs chew on the lemmings. Fritz throws Emery a rabbit leg,

"Tastes like lean chicken to you, I imagine. Except not roasted."

Emery smiles,

"Yeah, and chewy but grassy and earthy. I don't mind."

After chow time, the pack heads down and out of the deep forest and into a greener valley closer to the Ridgeline. They come across a ranch with volcanic rocks stacked up like a fort obviously made by humans. They trot around the rocks and find a black wolf chomping down on a turkey. He licks his chops and Fritz yells,

What are you doing, black rouge? If the humans catch you, they will skin you and make carpets out of your pelt!"

He smiles and licks his chops again. Emery realizes this is the mysterious wolf she saw when she left the pack for a few minutes.

The rouge snarls laugh, and chuckles,

"They'll shoot you anyway."

Fritz asks concerned,

"What pack are you with?"

"The rouge replies,

"I don't have a pack."

Emery kneels behind the Betas, taking cover from the outcast, and follows behind Fritz. He lifts his head and howls to pack.

"Let's be on our way, everyone!"

They trot out of the valley and back onto the trail. Emery keeps quiet about her previous encounter with the black rouge the day before...

An hour later they get back on the trail to the Ridgeline. Fritz teaches Emery,

"Never trust a lone wolf cast out of the pack! *We always stick together to the end and these rogues are usually cast out because they harm the pack.* He could have turned on his own kin, or even lead them astray?"

Emery nods in reassurance that she understands and keeps up with the pack. The next morning, they reach the Ridgeline and Emery thanks Fritz,

"I am grateful for your wisdom and have learned so much from you and the others. Please help us clear the ridges and valleys of mad goats and enjoy the feasting. I will return to my mother for now and revisit the pack next month. Look for Gregori circling high and listen for his call; he will screech three times on high and we shall meet near Silver lake below. Thank you, Charma and the rest of the pack, see you soon..."

Fritz thanks Emery and flashes her a few piercing teeth humorously,

"Happy Thanksgiving, Emery," and gathers his tribe for the mission.

Emery *shakes side to side vehemently and transforms* back into her young woman form. She runs her hands through her long blond hair, pushing it aside, preparing to return home.

Upon returning, she is greeted by her mother and some surprising guests over for dinner. Her mother turns to Emery,

"Emery, I am glad you are home. How was your day?"

Emery recalls leaving to explore in the forest this morning around 9:00 am but feels like she was gone for two weeks. She replies,

"Oh, I hiked up the North trail past the summit and saw a golden eagle and a couple coyotes." She replies nonchalantly.

Her mother glances at the guests, then Emery and replies,

"You have always been so adventurous, darling!"

"I would like you to meet our guests. This is our neighbor across the hill, John, the Rancher and his son, Guy."

Guy has a familiar look that Emery can't figure out. He has shiny black hair in contrast to light skin for a young man and radiant green eyes. *His mysterious gaze penetrates her briefly.*

John introduces himself,

"Hello, Emery sounds like a fun day...just be careful of those coyotes out there!"

Guy jumps in and laughs,

"Yeah...they'll team up and eat your sheep. I just shot one with my dad's rifle the other day!"

Emery's eyes widen...

"Come look at the valley with me," she indicates to Guy. They walk out to the back balcony.

"You see the border down there where the trees meet the pastures. The mad goats and wild sheep are eating the foliage and trees, stripping away all the shrubbery. The forest is dying down there."

Guy laughs,

"I think I like you as a wolf better..."

Emery pauses and replies,

"That was you, the black lone wolf?"

"Yes, a cunning canine, my curious she-wolf!"

Emery asks with skepticism,

"How could you?"

"What? Guy replies quickly."

"Eat a turkey, when the ranchers might shoot you?"

"No ranchers will shoot me! I am a Rancher's son. I was out there protecting our sheep from your friends"

Emery speaks up,

"My friends are keepers of the forest."

"Your friends are vicious thieves and have bottomless stomachs," Guy snaps back.

In the background Emery's mother and John, the rancher chuckle and giggle. She must teach the revealed rogue about the balance of nature. She can't have opposing forces. She whistles out into the ravine, echoing along screechy pitch that can be heard across the hills. A few minutes later, Grigori lands on her shoulder.

"Emery, you are back. Who do we have here?"

"This is Guy, the Rancher John's, son. He has revealed to me that he went rogue as a black wolf, and I saw him on our way back from Iceland."

"Never trust a lone wolf," Gregori advises.

Guy laughs. "Traveling alone is liberating and free. I can eat anything I want."

"Hold on to your fangs, *rogue wolf*. Let me explain something. The wolves keep the forest by keeping the grazers population in balance. They're our friends."

Guy defensively replies,

"But they eat my fathers' sheep."

Gregori's tongue hangs out for a second. "Not if you keep them fenced in and under control with your Aussie Shepard dog.

Emery nods and agrees with Gregori. He lifts both wings up and wraps them around the young human beings.

"It is time for you both to fly with me and I will show you the ways of the Keepers."

Emery lifts her arms, *shapeshifting* into her familiar Peregrine falcon form. She shares with Guy,

"Lift your arms and *imagine* a Peregrine falcon that looks like me!"

Guy slowly lifts his arms, focuses, and begins transforming into a falcon. Emery secretly is delighted to have a friend who understands her rare gift. Gregori leads the way,

"Soar with me, young lads. School is in session." They lift off the back deck of Emery's house and glide down into the ravine over Silver Lake. Gregori twists his golden-brown neck around and smiles, reaffirming his place in the forest. Gregori's flock of students has much to learn. He leads the flight around the perimeter of the lake showing them the landscape.

Not more than five minutes pass when suddenly Guy darts off to the right and swoops down onto the sandy shore swiftly snatching a rabbit with his newly found talons. He rips into the rabbit, tearing up its flesh and perches on top of a mossy pole and stuffs himself.

Emery is dumbfounded,

"You didn't ask Gregori to take a lunch break. We just got started. You're unbelievable, I like your human form better!"

Guy finishes devouring his rabbit, rubs his beak against his fur, and smiles at Emery and Gregori.

"I can really get into this predatory thing."

Emery replies,

"You can't help it; you have hunting in your blood."

Gregori reminds them,

"We only have two hours of daylight left, let's lift off!"

They take off from Silver Lake and fly over to the foggier,

colder side of the Ridge. Gregori swoops down over a nice meadow with Lavender Pines and circles a couple times above the purple trees. Guy and Emery ride his drift downward and upward through the air currents. Emery lines up behind his left wing and Guy behind his right. They form a triangular pattern and circle a few times.

Gregori sends out a high pitch screechy call as they circle....

Down below under the Lanvedars, Fritz appears and barks out a humorous call,

"Gregori, you old hoot, I knew you would show up soon and catch me near the Lavender."

Gregori replies,

"You know me too well. I can't help rubbing myself against these trees." Gregori lands on a lower branch of the Lavender Pines. Emery and Guy land on the branches next to his. Gregori turns his head side to side and then flutters his wings quickly in the purple branches. Purple pine needles blow off into the wind and all over his feathers.

"Ahh, I feel so alive! Nothing smells better than Lavender Pine..."

Fritz laughs,

"Ok, professor, what's the topic of class today?"

Gregori chuckles feeling profound and respected,

"MGV," he replies.

Fritz amused, inquires further,

"A new biological theory Eh?"

"Precisely, my alpha friend," Gregori responds.

Let me guess, "Megalomania Goat Virus?"

"Close, Fritz...I may use that one for another class topic. No, it's Mad Goat Virus."

Gregori turns to his class to ask,

"Any questions, birds?"

Emery and Guy lift their wings and whip some purple snow off their wings. Emery, inspired by sweet scent and wonderful Borealis in the sky offers,

"It's gone to their brains at the Ridgeline, the goats with MGV are the ones climbing the trees and eating the shrubbery."

And Guys jumps in,

"And I will catch and eat them all!"

"No, you won't," Fritz replied,

"We already ate most of them but there is one more heard of crazies we won't touch!"

Fritz continues,

"They have truly crazy looks in their eyes, so we won't eat those ones. We must come up with another plan."

Gregori turns to his eager class and challenges them,

"Any ideas, my shapely-humanoids?"

Emery lifts off into the air a foot or so and flaps her wings powerfully. Purple gusts fly off her wing tips...when she transforms back into her she-wolf form.

"Go Rogue and go black! Gregori follow me from above and Fritz lead with me!"

Emery howls and gathers the pack. Fritz encourages them alongside her. Guy changes back into his shifty rogue persona and joins Emery. Emery asks Fritz to take them to the mad goats,

"Ok, pack and shifters, let's find them!" Fritz takes them out of the meadow and over a small mountain range at the edge of the Ridgeline. They arrive at the barren trees and find a dozen tearing up all the lush green shrubbery. Emery lifts her nose, howls, and gathers the pack.

"Let's run them to the Cliffs of Insanity..."

She continues...

"Gregori, scare them from above out of the trees! Guy, flank around to the right side! And Fritz, get your pack to chase them off the cliffs. We will all drive them off the brink of *madness*..."

The Keepers and Shifters do their job, working together to chase the goats out of the trees. Fritz rallies the whole group and begins a march to the cliffs, pushing the crazies toward the jagged icy cliffs. They trot and sprint, marching the goats to the end of the green bluffs and off into the final edges of the world. The mad goats run to the end of the cliffs and have nowhere to go but off. They jump into the chasm of cold, dark nothingness and are gone forever.

"Well done!" Gregori congratulates Emery and flies back to his wonderful Lavender trees to flock around in a purple haze.

PSYLICON CAFÉ

"Hello, we would like a table for two."

"Hmm, did you reserve a spot on OpenTable?

"Um, no what is that?"

"Oh, my God, where have you been? It's only

The most popular dining reservation app out there today!"

"I'm sorry. We are from out of town, can you make an exception?"

"Oh, I guess."

"Today, we are having special, tectonic pancakes with info bytes on top."

"Wow sounds pretty dense dude...I don't know about that. Do you have any normal pancakes with fruit and yogurt?"

"I am not sure what you mean by normal, but we also have gigabyte sandwiches, oh, and yogurt with silicon wafer chips, sprinkled with hard-drive dust. Will that do?"

"I don't know... uh, honey what would you like? Does anything look tantalizing to you?"

"Yeah, I am curious about the hash tags with eggs? What's in that?"

"There's another favorite. We scramble Bitcoin eggs with pieces of social media sausage and potato tags. I recommend this dish cuz it really satisfies your add-a-friendly cravings."

"Ok, I'll take that," Lola responds reservedly.

Guy thinks about his choice. 'Where the hell are we, he wonders?'

"Fine, I'll take the Gigabyte sandwich."

The waiter leaves the table and Guy asks Lola,

"I enjoyed our morning hike through the Redwoods. It smells so fresh like new rain and Sequoia needles. What do you think of this place?"

Lola's eyes pinch inward. She slightly swipes her cheek. "I know, I was just picking strawberries under the redwood canopy and now I'm in techno-geek land, crazy..."

"I know," Guy reciprocates. "This whole valley used to be covered with apricot orchards. My dad told me he used to ride his bike through the orchards, chasing girls and playing baseball in the fields."

"Cool, my parents told me about the orange grottos where I am from in Goleta." My dad worked in a family run grocery store near the El Camino. He would gather up the oranges and bring them in and stock them daily."

Guy smiled. "How refreshing!"

The waiter brings the food out. Guy and Lola dive in and chow down. Halfway through their meal, Guy shares his thoughts,

"People around here seem wound-up pretty tight."

Lola nods,

"Yeah, they just want to accomplish a lot and succeed!" She shares confidently.

"I guess so, but at what cost?" Guy asks but obliges. Lola reaffirms her point,

"There's nothing wrong with wanting more out of life." Guy laughs,

"It's healthy to strive, but I prefer the natural way, it seems that people here are trying a little too hard..."

Lola's cheeks blush a bit and she shares,

"Well, maybe they just need to get out and take a nature hike more often like we just did."

"For sure!" Guy responds.

The waiter brings out a check-out-device for their bill with a touch screen and asks,

"Thank you for dining with us today at Psylicon Café', will you please complete a survey and pay here on our kiosk..."

Guy asks Lola,

"What do you think honey? How should we rate our brunch?"

Lola sarcastically responds,

I only ate it cuz I was so hungry from our hike."

"I know, me too." Guy agrees.

Guy fills out the survey with comments and the couple leaves the café' to continue their trip.

When the waiter comes back to the table to pick up the kiosk, the screen is frozen on the comments section and reads:

"Call tech support! Your hard drive crashed, the Bitcoin eggs got descrambled, the hash tags caught a potato virus, and there was a glitch in my Gigabyte sandwich..."

JAG RIGHT

June gloom looms today on the Santa Cruz coast. It's the type of cold you feel in your bone marrow, the kind of chill you will only tolerate when the waves are at least shoulder high, super quality, and barreling.

Thursday morning at 5:45 am the phone rings. I hang it up, it's way too early to get up. It rings again... I hang up. Another ring. Ok, I pick up.

"Why are you calling me this early Buffalo? Can you call me at 9:30," I ask?

"Just checked it, it's flatter than Lake Tahoe, Boxer and I are cruising over."

Buffalo and Boxer grab some tall Toots Coffee after checking the Hook and head over to my house. It's about a twenty-five-minute drive so they have time for chatting. Cruising in the slow Volvo, they barely make it up over the summit and as they drop down to town, Boxer dreams out loud,

"Buff, you think they'll ever make a wave-pool in a reservoir?" as he glances over at the Lexington Reservoir.

Buffalo replies, "On whose budget, braddah?" It would probably cost a couple million to install hydraulics and shape the bottom with the right topography and such."

Boxer follows up with another question, "How about one in Vasona Park for days like today during June gloom? We could all pitch in and put it on Hammer's credit card."

Buffalo laughs and nods, "It would be unreal."

They pull up in Buff's 1983 Volvo station wagon or the "Volvonic" as Buffalo calls it.

Da Braddahs cruise over the hill to chill here in the land where the palms meet the pines in the den of the wildcats nestled in the southwestern foothills of Silicon Valley

We call it "The Valley," or "The Oven" because you can experience a twenty-degree difference in temperature from the ocean. These micro-climates are unique and amazing and give us an advantage with options when the June-July fog gets thick on the coast.

Temperatures have been pushing 98 degrees Fahrenheit lately and we've been hunkering down in the air conditioning, watching surf movies like *Blazing Boards* from the 1980s and raiding my dad's fridge. We also spend a good amount of the day swimming and lounging at the local Swim & Racquet Club pool. While sprawled out on the pool deck later that afternoon, we notice a couple of kids bring their Super Soaker water guns to the pool. These kids, maybe middle-school aged, are having the best time of anyone around. Leave it up to big kids to learn from the smaller ones. Johnny Boy, the biggest kid in our crew suggests,

"Guys let's go buy some Super Soakers. No one's having as much fun as these kids."

I figure why not. It's scorching hot, summertime and homework is miles away from my mind. So, we drive over to the drugstore and buy a couple Super Soakers and go back to the pool. Boxer rips one out of the package and Johnny Boy opens the other. They start a water blasting battle that takes them all over the pool, on the deck, running through the grass, in the men's locker room, and even shooting the lifeguards accidentally, I hope?

"Guys, we're going to get booted if you don't chill out!"

Boxer turns and yells, "No worries," and then squirts the honey-lifeguard right in the face. Johnny Boy jumps into the madness and shoots her a couple times as well. The lifeguard shouts sarcastically,

"You guys are probably in your early twenties and you're worse than those kids. Knock it off." Boxer and Johnny Boy calm it down for a few brief minutes. Buffalo and I are kicking it on the lounge chairs.

Buffalo pulls out a huge stack of 5" x 7" notecards that are color-coated perfectly and asks me to quiz him on his GRE (Graduate Record Exam) vocabulary words.

I interject, "Dude, this has to be a 1000-word stack?"

He replies, "Well, that's only a small fraction of the words I have to know for the test!"

I begin, "Okay, here's one, "Jag."

"What a piece of cake" I comment.

Buffalo confidently answers, "as a noun, it's a sharp edge, but as a verb, it means to go on a non-stop drinking binge like Boxer last night. Oh, and there's a third meaning as a verb, to jerk quickly."

"Nice, I didn't realize the secondary and tertiary connotations."

Meanwhile, Boxer keeps squirting the girl lifeguard, probably acting out his fantasy crush on the poolside *Bay Watcher*. So, I pull the plug and rally the guys to go home for some barbecue.

We return home and cue up some barbecue chicken and stuff ourselves silly. We watch a few surf movies then feel like going out in the hot summer night. At age twenty we are stuck between the party world and the bar life. We are too young for the bars and sick and tired of the same ole neighborhood parties.

Boxer blurts out a brilliant idea,

"Let's fill the Super Soakers and head downtown to carouse. After all, it's 84 degrees tonight anyway, right?"

I remember how much fun we had a few summers back in Palm Springs for spring break when we got squirt guns and filled them with water and invisible ink that would change colors when sprayed on college girls. The only problem was we had to get close enough to them to share our colorful expressions of admiration. The Beastie Boys song, "Brass Monkey" was blaring out of every other low rider truck with an insane display of auto gymnastics, hydraulics, pumps, breaks, beeps, etc.

We all pile into the *Volvonic* with Buffalo driving and Boxer riding shotgun. Johnny Boy and I position ourselves nicely in the back seat. Boxer has a fully water-loaded Super Soaker at room temperature ready to fire and keeps it under wraps by the floor mats near his feet. Johnny Boy recommends with a higher intelligence that we drive downtown on the strip at the local bar hang out.

"Let's roll down North Santa Cruz Blvd. and see what the honeys are up to..."

Buffalo drops into town and approaches the strip of bars. The first is *Last Call*, nothing there, boring. It's at the end of the strip anyway. Next is our friendly local Irish pub, *CB Hannegans* but is sort of tucked away down the street with not too much excitement, so we keep rolling...

Boxer spots a nice line at the *Black Watch* and yells out, "over there, look at the girls. Nice! Buff, slow down."

Boxer lifts the Super Soaker and points it out the window and aims for the two girls in line but hits one of the only bad-ass, cowboy-looking guys in line. This guy has Wrangler jeans, kick-ass cowboy boots, a button up red range shirt and an authentic looking Stetson hat.

"Oh Shoots, Boxer you nailed the cowboy in line at the end," I exclaimed.

We all look at each other and scream, "NO...."

Johnny Boy commands, "Floor it, Buff!" Buffalo short circuits for a second then hit the gas. The cowboy starts sprinting toward the back-right corner of the *Volvonic*.

"More gas Buff!" I yell.

Buffalo accelerates to about eight miles per hour and gets some distance between the cowboy, and us but we approach a red at the next stoplight. The cowboy gets about fifteen feet from grabbing the car and I shout,

"Jag Right!"

Buffalo slows to turn right at the intersection. The cowboy reaches the *Volvonic* and slaps the car and gets a hold of Johnny Boy's *TEAM SUGAR* green T-shirt that Boxer made for all of us. He rips the shirt in half and takes it with him but loses steam a bit as Buffalo accelerates out of the turn. We gain momentum and get away further down the road. The cowboy threatens us with a few screams,

"Dip-shits, I'll get you guys!"

He slowly fades away in the rear-view mirror and we make our way through the mountain roads and return to my house. We all sigh with relief and Buffalo laughs,

"All those seemingly meaningless hours of studying vocab words sure paid off, Hammer. *Jag Right*. Classic."

SAVING CANDOR

Andrew was as pure as they came. At age nineteen, he hadn't kissed a girl, drank a beer, and most likely, never slandered a soul. He often had a glazed look on his face like nothing ever bothered him.

"Hey, Dom, you know, that sandy blonde girl in our chemistry class, Jen, I think her name is. I wonder what it would be like to kiss her?"

Dom scratches his chin for a second and replies to Andy,

"She looks like the kind, if you kiss her right, she will love you forever. She probably has a close family, loves Daddy, and eats blueberry pie." He further encourages,

"Andy, you should ask her out... so we can double date this weekend."

"How should I ask her?"

"Tell her your friend, Dom is having people over at his girlfriend's house and that you'd like her to come."

"Good idea, I'll do that." Andy is quick to please his company no matter what they ask. He is simple and easy to hang with.

Friday rolls around. Dom and Lisa are chilling at her house, drinking a beer when Andy (*Mr. Smiles)* walks in with his new companion, the sweet Jen.

"Dom & Lisa, this is Jen. We have chemistry together... I mean we have a chemistry class."

Dom chuckles a bit amused at Andy's Freudian slip. Dom replies, "Hey Jen, this is Lisa." They exchange "Hellos"

"You guys want to see the house? It's an old Victorian," Lisa adds.

"Dom loves this house because it's big, spacious, and stocked with lots of frozen dinners in the fridge!"

They all walk up the stairs to her room.

"This is the walk-in closet." Lisa points to the enormous space. She then proceeds into the bathroom. I hear a musical tune and turn around. Andy is strumming on a guitar he just picked up.

"Sounds like a familiar Clapton song?" Dom asks.

"Yep," he answers.

"Old Love," Jen confirms.

Andy keeps playing. Meanwhile, Lisa shows them her room and the backyard. The girls walk down the stairs and keep chatting. Dom stays and listens to Andy jamming. He is excellent!

"Where'd you learn that?"

"I've been playing for about ten years. Being stuck up on that hill leaves a lot of time for playing music." Andy transforms from chemistry nerd to *Smooth Daddy* to Eric Clapton...all in one week!

"That reminds me... Dom, could I stay at your house for a few nights?"

"Sure, I have a 1970's style sofa bed rigged up with the view of the bay! You can camp there. We can cram for the big chemistry test on Thursday; we'll get super caffeinated, have a cram session, then ace it."

The boys cruise back down to the living room to get a few beers.

"Have a Sierra Nevada Pale Ale," Dom offers both Andy and Jen a beer. Dom is curious if Andy will accept in front of Jen, his new date.

Andy obliges and takes his first swig like he's Frat Boy of the Year. His eyes tingle and then tear over his reddened cheeks. Dom was happy to see him relax and lighten up a little socially. It was a pleasure enjoying the company of new friends.

Next Monday after class, the boys cruise over to Dom's house, start a fire, brew up a pot of coffee, and dive into chemistry. The only way to pass chemistry is to buddy up, get Geeked out of your mind, and push each other to pile through the material.

Dom inquires, "So, why aren't you going back up there, on the hill?"

"They won't let me back up there, now that I've left."

"Dam, that's pretty harsh," Dom exclaims.

"You ready to start a new life down here, in the real world?"

"Yep, I'm nineteen and it's time to wake up and see the world!" Andy answers with anticipation in his eyes.

"You're getting a great start, you know, going out with Jen and drinking your first beer."

Dom encourages.

"Well, let's get started on this stuff. Open up to the ideal gas law: $PV=nRT$, the formula of the night."

"What's the relationship between pressure and volume?" Dom asks Andy.

"They're inversely related. In a closed system, as pressure goes up, volume goes down and vice versa." Andy confidently answers.

"Good, my boy, we're off to a good start; let's do problems 1-5."

They work out the problems and move to a new section- *Entropy*:

"A measure of randomness; the tendency for energy to scatter into disorder," Dom states.

"Hey Dom, entropy makes me think of my dog. I haven't seen him in so long," Andy mumbles.

"What's his name?"

"Candor... He's a good dog, an Australian Shepherd; he always does what I say and is very loyal. I can depend on him to scare away raccoons and mountain lions and he always alerts me of any danger. One time the neighbor's dog broke into our trash bin, and I tried to shoo him off, but he bit my foot. Candor came to the rescue and slapped him on the ass."

"Andrew, since you miss Candor so much, why don't we rescue him from the snare of the devil?" Dom suggests.

"Yeah, I have been thinking about how to get him back. If I could get him back, I could take him to my mother's house in Santa Cruz, and he'd be perfectly safe there."

Dom continues with his proposal,

"I've got it, I know exactly what to do. We dress up in night commando gear and take him tonight," he says boldly.

The boys were truth-seekers on a mission to save the dog that represents peace to Andy. He smiles with a smirk of worldly intent and confidence. Andy's large candid smile shrinks to a vengeful grin. Dom provides him the push he needs to follow through and reclaim his dog held captive.

"We're on, let's do it," Andy replies. The boys dress in black sweatshirts and camouflage and head up the mountain.

Dom pulls his hood over his head and wraps his sleeves around his hands to keep out the cold air that enters the car window as they drive closer to their destination.

"Where is this community?" Dom asks.

"It's at Lakefront, up by Skyline Road" Andy replies.

"How many people live up there?"

"About two hundred and growing. My dad's wife, Jean, keeps convincing people to move up there," Andy answers.

"Who's in charge?"

"She is," Andy mumbles.

"How can that be? Dom asks with skepticism. I thought the Bible indicates that men should lead churches. At least I haven't run into a woman pastor yet in my long nineteen years of life..."

The old grin grew right back on Andy's honest face.

"I know, she seems to be making her own rules up," Andy explains.

"It all started back in the garden with that shiny apple, right Andy?" Dom jokes. Andy appreciates Dom's rare, harsh humor, as his upbringing wouldn't allow it.

Andy adds, "She even tried to tell me who to marry and that I was going to be a doctor, of course."

"This woman sounds like a crazy Jezebel trying desperately to grasp control of her own life through the poor lives of others," Dom proclaims.

The boys pile into Dom's white 4-Runner. Dom turns the heater on full blast to fight the piercing chill creeping into his truck. The boys now approach the densely populated redwood forest. The Redwoods stand boldly like lions protecting the domain of a king, a most powerful king. They keep out cars, tractors, and other civilized encroachments that tend to spoil the forest. Dom rolls down the window for a second to air the truck out and smell the damp forest permeates the truck, reminding him of divinity and supreme creation. Dom points out a shooting star across the sky that lights up the forest for a brief second. The star shooting in the direction of their destination...

As they drive to the top of the mountain the boys chat,

"My dad's wife once said she saw Jesus in a redwood tree, and that he told her to start this community up here in the forest," Andy shares with Dom.

"Beware of those who say they see Jesus in a tree he thought, 'From the book of Matthew I think.' Or something like, you know a tree from the fruit it bears..."

Then Dom voices to Andy,

"Doesn't the book of Matthew discuss the notion about not trusting people who say they see Jesus in a tree?"

"I'm not sure, but my dad's wife once did say she saw Jesus in a tree."

Dom is appalled. She appears to be the one protecting such lies, a definite wolf in sheep's clothing.

Andy continues, "I'm bummed that my father got involved with her; she talked him into moving up here and joining them."

That must be difficult to deal with," Dom consoles Andy.

"They spent one year in house-arrest for false imprisonment of two kids in the church. They kept them in the basement for a year, complaining that the children were defiant and incorrigible."

"Where were the parents during all of this?" Dom asks.

"The parents went to Europe on an outreach program, and when they returned, the kids told them what happened and they charged my dad and stepmom with false imprisonment," Andy explains.

"No way," Dom fires-up more motivation to help. Hypocrisy is smoldering in the forest, and we are here to put an end to this injustice." Dom encourages with exuberance.

"About a year after serving their time, Jean started developing a brain tumor, and it's been growing ever since," Andy adds.

Dom envisions a grotesque silhouette of the elephant man, Joseph Merrick style (from the movie, *Elephant Man*).

As they approach the commune, Andy wrestles in his seat.

"Are you nervous?" Dom asks.

"A little, but I won't feel bad for taking him back. I am his best friend, anyway."

After driving five miles of winding road, the boys come to a stop about a hundred yards from Andy's old house. Dom parks below the house next to some trees to lay low. The night is cold and dark and only glimpses of light slice through the treetops and little pieces of midnight blue trickle through. The boys watch a bit and talk for a while.

"My dad joined what, I guess, he thought it was a tight church group. Turns out... Jean started coercing members to move up to Lakefront Properties. She had them sell their previous houses and invest in the commune. She pretty much monopolized the whole property. Next thing you know, she's dictating rules to members." Andy continues to share his disappointing experiences for the last sixteen years of his life.

"Jean even had other guys spank me with a plank when I did something wrong," Andy said quietly with a horrific look in his eyes.

This story was growing as fast as cancer in Jean's brain. Dom shares his inner beliefs with Andy,

"Let someone dark get a hold of feeble people and entropy will take over completely. That's entropy, the scattering of atoms and the tendency of chaos to win. Now you are away from them and soon you will be with your dog! Meanwhile, Jean's head is swelling like a water balloon and your act of love slows a little of that dark entropy down. You can heal the disease of chaos by saving one last piece of good that is left, Candor!"

The clock reads 11:25 pm.

"They'll fall asleep around 11:30 pm and then we can sneak in around 12:00 and snatch Candor from the pit of despair," Andy told Dom.

Diabolic darkness in the forest envelops the boys. All Dom could think of was that Merrick like head. All that extra-alien like cerebral cortex where it doesn't belong (on a human's head at least). *Pressure goes up and volume won't hold, it decreases, and no one can change the law of physics.* The brains must go somewhere. Out the ears maybe, bulging through the eyes, right out the orbital foramina. Whenever it may be, these laws written above don't change. Gravity holds these stars visible to our eyes in place. We are on a spot here on Earth where we are limited to spatial order. The kind of order that keeps the planets aligned and people grounded in the soil here on earth.

"Ok, it's 11:59, let's change. Vamos con Dios," Dom whispers, "Andy, you lead hombre; I'll be in your shadows."

Andy shuffles up to the first redwood on the front lawn. Dom follows right behind him. They make themselves skinny to hide any bit of their bodies that can be seen from the second floor where Andy's dad and Jean are sleeping.

"Look, Dom," Andy whispers silently.

"My dad's asleep, but she's still awake."

Andy points to the window. With a soft light on in the background, they see a dark figure pacing back and forth across the room. The figure stops and gazes out the window for a second and then turns to pace again. In the silhouette, a large round bump in the shape of a croissant bulges on her head like Joseph Merrick's.

"Candors over there in the backyard by the neighbor's house. follow me." Dom scurries behind Andy like a stranger in an unknown land.

"Candor," Andy lightly calls. The friendly shepherd runs up and gives his lost buddy a good lick. The boys run back to the street with Candor following them. Andy opens the door and lets the dog in.

"You're with me now for good," Andy reassures his dog as he hugs him with relief and satisfaction.

The boys jump back in the truck and bring Candor back with them to Dom's house for the night. Dom congratulates Andy for taking back his dog and reclaiming some of that *chaos* that separated them. The adventurous undergrads were able to slow *entropy* a bit and re-establish some emotional order in Andy's life.

Dom didn't see Andy for two years, after that night, until he ran into him at a local coffee shop. Andy shared with him that he was attending a university in San Diego and that he regularly played guitar at coffee shops. He had a girlfriend, and they would probably get married soon. Dom asks about his dad and Jean. Andy replies nonchalantly as always,

"Jean's head exploded from the tumor and my dad left the cult. He's living peacefully down in Santa Cruz." They talked for a short while and Dom gave him a hug and finished off with, "Well, that's great everything worked out, it's funny how life works, huh?"

"Yep," and he went on his happy way.

ISLAY'S VISION

Mountains blanketed in gold, sleep soundly near the undefined line of the nine gatekeepers of Lucia, capturing any sea-wolfs daring upon the land. These wayfarers end up as prey caught in the nets of maids woven by their mother, Ran. The sisters net the pirates and turn them upside down, shaking them violently to empty their sticky pockets of stolen loot.

They daisy chain the loot from the marshy sea to sister and sister until the ninth one, Islay, unloads the treasure in the land of bishops, where their father Egir plans a grand party for the nobles. He will brew the finest ale for the monks of the new world, a Christianized world of one God that reigns in the warm valley of Eden. Egir offers gold and iron to the Chumash for their help in gathering coastal live oak acorns, sagebrush, and sticky monkey flowers to make the ale. Egir knows not the land but the sea and offers his elves and dwarfs to aid the monks who work night and day at making giant oak barrels to brew the ale.

Egir calls on Thor to deliver stormy seas with lightning bolts toward Eden. He mixes the ingredients into the large barrels and recovers a lightning rod from the mast of a wrecked Franciscan ship and electrifies the ale with his charged rod, mixing and brewing the grog. After work, guarding the seashore, his nine daughters test the brew and chime in. Morro speaks first, "Father, it's too bitter, it needs more Monkeyflower. Madonna adds, "I like the sagebrush with its fruity aftertaste, I recommend more of that for the finest elixir…father!"

Egir thanks his daughters,

"I appreciate the smooth palate's, girls! Your mother tastes fish in everything she tries. It helps to have nine opinions!" Speaking of Ran, where is your mother, ladies?"

Suddenly, a wave from the sea rolls over the hills and Ran appears with her mouth wide open, releasing the sea back over the hills like a giant surge in the tides through the marshes and to the ocean. As Ran opens her mouth to speak, some salmon jumps out of her mouth into her net. Egir spears it with his trident and swallows it like a seafood appetizer. Ran turns to her daughter Islay,

"Islay, my prophetic darling, have you shared your latest dream with the monks and Chumash?"

Islay shakes off her green viny coat of grapes, stands tall, and peers across Eden and chants like a seeress from the sea,

"When I close my misty eyes, I see a beautiful garden of green, turned swampy with steam if I were not to share my dream. If our nations dare not speak to share a common ground in a land where oceans awake and get angry with waves that have sound, we must join, *Chumash, Franciscan, and Norse.* For if we miss this time to dine in the West in Eden…. tales no more will be told of mountains of gold, plump purple grapes, and coastal live oaks…. no more, will acorns adorn, falcons dive, nor will the vines make fine wines. This land I shall say will be swept up by the sea and become barren and dull."

Father Francisco thanks Islay for her vision with an important message to the settlers and reassures his position as a Father with a Mission for his people in the land of bishops,

"Our father has delivered us to this land with a message for all! To establish a church in the valley at this post along the golden coast where we may pay reverence to the one GOD who rules all. The GOD of Spain, the Lord of the New World, and the Father of the valley of Eden and land of the nobles."

Chief Mowak of the Chumash speaks up in his Salinan-English pidgin,

"Islay, we receive your message as gatekeeper of the Water World and gladly accept your gesture like we do mother ocean's seashells for our culture and trade. Father Francisco, we listen and hear your talk from the Sky World of one nation joined together under one GOD in the sky...with all good purpose we intend to share our trade and goodwill to live together here in the Middle World on the land we stand."

Chief Mowak nods over to one of his daughters, Cheewak who opens a leather satchel and gives Father Franciscan a beautiful necklace with beads from the grasslands and blue and red shells from the sea. Father Francisco thanks them and promises to teach them the ways of the Christian GOD in the Sky. He further offers jobs of building missions of brick and stone from the earth and proclaims them as holy places of worship to the one true GOD in the sky.

Chief Mowak obliges with open arms and reminds the people of the land that he will have his oldest daughter, Feena whose spirit animal is the mountain lion, watch over the lands of his nation.

That afternoon, the nation's join at the floor of the valley near the river springs that flow through Eden. Each nation and their representatives dine together at Egir's party and drink of his transformational elixir and anticipate sharing the land with each other and how best to survive and protect this lush garden that lies nestled along the nine sisters, marching toward the sea.

BLUE SPRINGS

After swimming from sea to sea on his one-thousand-year quest for love, Proteus sends a request to Poseidon for help on his journey.

"Neptune, I have surfed every wave in every sea that bears a storm and have yet to find my maiden."

King Neptune swirls his trident; bubbles spiral around and propel up toward the surface. He has Proteus meet him at the base of the Aegean's underwater coliseum.

"If you haven't found your aqua-mate in your thousand-year search, maybe you should try your luck on earth. There is a spring in the land of Helena where you may relinquish your tail for legs."

In awe, Proteus' eyes widen the size of sand dollars.

The King of the Sea unwraps layer upon layer of seaweed from an embedded sea-scroll like a book from an old dusty library. He flips through the soggy pages and finds a passage in the chapter on land laws that states,

"Pisces who fail at finding aqua-mates during their thousand-year swim must embark on a land journey where earth, land, and fire meet near the vineyards in the valleys of Helena where hot springs spew blue."

He reads further through the barnacle-laden book and finds a chapter on fine wine. Poseidon turns to Proteus and commands him to bring back some aged Helena wine after he finds his mate.

Neptune continues,

"Rich flavorful wines can't ferment overnight but take many land years to mature. So, I encourage you to search Helena's valleys patiently. I've had enough sea cucumber ale to last me many moons, Ha Ha... burp. (Bubbles)"

Proteus wonders about the elements needed to develop wine. He reads on...

"Without the bright light to heat up the vine, you can't get fine wine."

Hmmm...for grapes to flourish and thrive in Helena's land the sun must blanket the valley of grapes to capture the heat that helps the vines climb up mountain peaks and then cool at night in the misty sea vapor.

Proteus reads on...

" To find purple grapes the size of plums, swim beyond the giant gates of gold, all the way through the marshes and rivers to the mountains of blue steam. You must journey inland for miles to reach Helena."

Proteus heeds Neptune's advice and embarks on his love journey. He swims from the Aegean Sea to Atlantia and across the warm bath waters of the Gulf of Americas. As he leaves the Gulf and swims through the Panama Canal into the Pacific, he feels a chill like never. His gills contract a little, but he shutters it off and continues north along the Western American plate and the deep into the frigid Pacific.

As he leaves the Isthmus of Panama, Proteus rides the South Equatorial Currents north like a liquid escalator up to California. As he approaches Baja, he fights the headwaters from California currents sucking him down to the bottom with high pressure. He manages to get closer to the shore where he gets pushed up by the buffer from the coastal backwash and undertow.

He swims for days and hours trying to find the intertidal currents that push off the landmass north against the head currents. Three days up to the coast he swims into a harbor that appears to have a bridge or gate over the top but is a dull grey and not gold. He breaks from his swim and hides on the inside of the harbor and notices two large towers with vapor steaming out from the top. Sea lions bark at him and boats pass him frequently. He takes one more look for the giant gates of gold and sees none so decides to keep on swimming north. He scales the edge of the sea canyon along the sand-spit dunes.

The next day he approaches a huge bay that opens larger than any he has seen on the coast. He pops his head up high searching for the giant gates but sees only cool dense vapor. He keeps on swimming north for another ten miles and rests in a small bay with a jetty with nice waves rolling in. He needs to swim in closer to get a better look at the shoreline.

Then he feels a drop in the sea level and a surge upward over a swell. He looks at the horizon and sees lines of swells stampeding toward him like giant green corduroy in 70s style jeans. He thrusts his powerful tail twice and streamlines headfirst into a feathery gem that peels all the way in.

On the inside shelf, a surfer girl paddles into his wave and catches it on the surface. She smacks the lip, carves a smooth cut back, and while cranking her board around the whitewash, notices a shadow in her wave below her. She glances over her left shoulder and keeps shredding the wave up. As she straightens out down the line to race the inside section, Proteus looks up at the somewhat stiff fish on the surface with rainbow colors and bumps it out of the water. The surfer girl flies off her board and into the water directly in front of Proteus. He darts to the right to miss her, but his huge fishtail slaps her side.

Proteus stops swimming and surfaces; his green and gold reflective tail curves up behind him. The surfer girl sits up on her board almost shocked out of her wetsuit! She screams,

"What? Where did you come from and where did you get that big tail? My girlfriend in Hawaii has one of those and swims with it at Waimea Bay when it's flat."

Proteus responds awkwardly,

"This, this... is me, it's all me, naturally!"

The girl jumps in,

"Come on, and it's too cold to be out here without a suit."

Proteus pauses for a few seconds and then replies,

"Yes, I have never been colder... it's nothing like Atlantia, my gills keep contracting and my scales are tight!"

The girl jokes,

"I feel like I'm watching an episode of Mako Mermaids, only... it feels kind of real, without an Australian accent.... More of an old English dialect. Is this a prank?"

Proteus proclaims to the dumbfounded surfer girl,

"I am Proteus of the Aegean Sea on a search for my mate in the land of Helena!"

Theatrically entertained, the girl reciprocates,

"I am Brianna of Bolinas and can nose ride longer than any terrestrial here on earth!"

Proteus speaks up,

"I am seeking the bay with gates of gold to guide me to the land of Helena. Can you take me there?"

Brianna laughs and jokes,

"You swam 10 miles too far north. But I can show you how to get to the 'gates of gold' as you call them. She asks another question, "Isn't the land of Helena in Greece?"

He confidently responds,

"The sacred sea-scroll has it written that I am to journey to the land in the Americas where springs spew blue."

And he further adds,

"Nowhere in the Aegean can I find the blue springs. You must take me there and I will pay you in silver drachmas."

Proteus reaches into a large-scale pouch near his waistline and shows Brianna a silver drachma. You can see the silver reflect from her eyes as she lights up with wonder. Brianna seizes the opportunity, as she needs art supplies for her next masterpiece...

"Follow me to shore"

Brianna paddles into the cove by the beach.

Proteus follows behind but slows near the shallows.

Brianna smiles and jokes,

"Ok, you can lose the merman tail. I will drive you to the gates of gold."

Shocked and confused, Proteus replies,

"As I told you earlier, my tail is real! Straight from Atlantis in the Aegean Sea. Come here, feel for yourself."

Now in knee high deep water, Brianna approaches Proteus slowly. He cleeks and clacks quickly as a joke (sounds like a dolphin sound).

"Ha, ha" he chuckles amused.

She gently swipes his tail gently with the back side of her right hand and pushes deeper into his thruster and he cleeks again...

Brianna pauses and freezes for a moment. She smiles in wonder as if she discovers a unicorn. Her eyebrows rise in mystery,

"My girlfriend's mermaid's tail is made of rubber-like swim fins...

And this truly feels real."

He reassures her by raising it up five feet and slapping the water powerfully like a whale tail.

Brianna stands back and marvels at her appealing fish friend.

Proteus takes the opportunity to educate her on ancient mythological teachings,

"Poseidon's sea scroll teaches us that we may relinquish our tail for legs if we find the land where springs spew blue in Helena."

Brianna replies in a witty tone,

"Why would you want to give up your fins for legs? I can't get enough time in the water and by the way, I would love to go to Atlantis!"

She carries on...

"I am sculpting a statue of Poseidon out of sand and coral."

Brianna suggests that Proteus meet her at Sea Glass Beach, eleven miles south of her point break.

"Can you meet me eleven nautical miles south of here tomorrow at 10:30 am Pacific time. You will see a huge bay where the gates of gold stand bright orange and bold in the misty fog. Don't go into the bay but stop on the beach before it with the brilliant iridescent sea glass that has replaced the sand. If you reach the bay, you have gone too far south."

Proteus obliges,

"I will be there Brianna of Bolinas"

Proteus hunkers down in a cold undersea shelf on the edge of Bolinas Bay for the night.

Brianna returns home and marvels and imagines possibilities with her new friend.

Next morning Proteus swims with the northwest currents down to the mouth of the gates of gold. He peers up and marvels at the huge radiant structures of orange and wonders how they stay up and stand so high above the ocean level. He is surprised at the tremendous height, as he hasn't experienced any structures above the water that high.

He scans the mini bays before the bay and finds a colorful iridescent rainbow effect illuminating through the fog. He lifts his head and calculates the sun angle inclination and sizes up a 35°/145° 10:30 Pacific Time alignment.

Brianna is on shore near a green glass ramp that rises to the kaleidoscope looking beach. A small dingy metal boat is tied to a Monterrey Cypress tree trunk.

She waves him up the smooth glass ramp with a lattice texture to it but smooth enough for any seal or fish to slide on. He slips right up to the sparkling purple dock. An iridescent rainbow hovers over them like some far away land.

"What do you think?" She asks.

Proteus replies with surprise,

"Never have I seen rocks, shoreline, or sand as colorful with brilliance as this."

Brianna motions to the right,

"Follow me."

Proteus slips, flips, and slides across the transparent platform down a slide to an opening along the cliffside.

"Check out my glass house. I made it from bottles adrift and washed up ashore here on Sea Glass Beach."

Proteus easily slips over the smooth glassy bottom beach. Brianna shuffles toward the bottom of the cliff where a small cave of about sixty feet is carved out of the hillside. Proteus follows.

Brianna secretly smiles and brings Proteus to the bottom of the cave and steps into a small iridescent multi-color glass house. Behind the house, a brilliant rainbow displays on the edge of the rocky cliff from light refracted off the sea and sunlight through Brianna's masterful creation.

"Check out my glass beach house!"

These are my glass sculptures. Some are sea glass and others are in sand and coral."

Proteus smiles and appreciates this,

"Wow, you sculpted Neptune! Whoa..."

Proudly she informs Proteus,

"Yeah, I did that one out of a large piece of coral I collected from Anini Beach in Kauai."

Proteus marvels at the giant coral and comments,

"I haven't seen a coral head big enough to even think of carving such a wonderful piece as this."

Brianna replies that she makes regular trips to Kauai to visit her friends and surf in contests on the North Shore.

She asks further,

What do you think of my surf shack? I have been putting this together for the last two years...

"I started with a base of blue and purple and added reds and yellows as I went up so light can get in"

Proteus gazes at the blue sea glass around the window frames and remembers why he is here.

"Have you been where springs spew blue?"

Brianna scratches her head puzzled,

"The only springs I know of are in Calistoga, and Big Sur but they aren't blue. Just clear with bubbles and wonderful...

I would take you there but how would we get you there without water?"

"The sea scrolls states that the land of Helena has Blue Springs where I may get legs as I mentioned earlier."

Brianna remembered when she was on her last surf trip to Kauai, she discovered a cave that had blue water but no springs. Later she realizes the cave is an old hollowed out lava tube with light reflecting out as blue light and the water is not truly blue but an illusion. She assumes blue water must be found deep down in caves underground. Brianna comes up with an idea,

"Proteus, you said your book in Atlantis instructs you to go to the land of Helena by passing through the gates of gold. Well, let us travel by boat through the gates of gold and up the delta in search of your blue springs. You can swim along with my boat incognito, and I will guide you to your mysterious land. We can leave tomorrow. Meet me here again tomorrow morning at 7:00 am so we may sneak through the bay...

Proteus slept in the glass house that night and woke up to Brianna greeting him with a big smile. She arrives bundled up in a green and black jacket and has rope in her hand.

"Good morning! Let's get moving before the fog burns off."

She ties the rope to the back of her boat and leaves about thirty feet of slack for Proteus.

"You can hang on to this if the currents get strong near the gate and the straits at the mouth and around the islands."

Proteus laughs,

"I will be fine. Especially after making it through the straits down at the bottom of the American continent. I'll be ok."

Brianna throws him the rope and they launch off the sea-glass beach into the currents near the mouth of the bay. He hangs on tight as Brianna accelerates her trusty little boat into the mouth of the bay. He thrusts his tail fin smoothly as they motor under the bridge and past a small island on the left. A group of small harbor seals follow them, jumping and playing along with the wake of the boat. No one notices them because the early morning fog blurs their presence to other boaters.

Proteus dives down below the boat when another vessel cruises by, keeping himself hidden deep in the cold bay water. They pass two small islands and approach shallower waters with kelp and seaweed. Occasionally, he maneuvers around the thick brown kelp. He isn't used to the strength of the kelp here in the North Pacific waters. Back home most of the seaweed is deep underwater and eaten as a salad for dinner by the Aegean.

Brianna checks with Proteus occasionally,

"How are doing back there?" She asks curiously.

"Aside from the kelp sandwich, I'm fine. The visibility isn't so great but I'm fine."

As they enter the San Pablo Bay Brianna asks Proteus,

"Want to join me up here in the boat for a while?"

He obliges.

"My counselor Helen advised me to go on twenty dates and find a winner. She thinks I will find the right fit." Brianna pauses for a second and then laughs,

"If you had legs, you could be my first!"

Proteus smiles.

"Brianna of Bolinas, I would be honored to be your first suitor if we can find the land where springs spew blue."

They stopped for gas in Benicia near the huge Navy boats. Proteus remembers seeing a few of these back in Greece when they passed through to Europe years ago. He recalls encountering the submarines and dodging torpedoes.

"A long time ago I saw this ship near my homeland." He shares with Brianna.

"This one here launched a few torpedoes that I had to dodge rapidly; I lost a few scales from that one!" He recalls the disturbing experience.

Brianna adds,

"This is the mothball fleet that's just collecting dust and mothballs, I guess." You won't see these in Greece anymore. They just lie here and rust and are a home for birds and raccoons.

The land and sea couple dock over at the edge of San Pablo Bay and fuel up.

Brianna reminds Proteus to stay low,

"Remember to stay low."

He agrees and ducks down.

After marveling at mankind's creation and madness, the sea-goers turn north into the Napa River more upstream into the narrow, muddier water flow. Proteus spits out a few mouth-full of water and swims out toward the center of the river to dilute out the muddy banks.

After another hour or so they come upon a warm fervent green valley with big rocks in a circular fashion like an old volcano. In the middle of the lush valley spouts of hot water and steam shoot up in the air. The river narrows more and dead ends at a pool where a rusty orange and yellow ring circle around a large spout of steamy, hot spring water.

Brianna inquires,

"Do you think this is where springs spew? We must be close. "

Proteus agrees.

"I remember another passage from the sea scroll book that read....

'On the hunt for Mt. Helena you will find where she spouts living holy water from the veins of the earth for those that need rejuvenation'

They make it down to the main spout and find an earthy female statue standing under the spring with her arms outstretched as if she is waiting for someone. She's robed in old graying ivory like a mortar with a laurel in her hair. She has a concerned stare like she is eternally waiting to help a lost soldier. Her left hand is pointing in a direction toward a cave in the ground at the end of the pool.

Brianna grabs Proteus' hand and shows him the "hot spot" where spring water spews up from the core... at this point, he is in about four feet of water and almost dry-docked...with less hydrated scales. His tail begins drying out...

Brianna follows Helena's hand and seizes Proteus' hand,

"Come with me down to the pools."

He follows her. She steps into the warm reinvigorating sulfurous pools.

They bathe in the nutritious waters. Soft sulfur penetrates Proteus' skin down to the bone, relaxing his sore and tired tail fin from his journey.

While in the healing waters they embraced each other firmly. Proteus asks Neptune to grant him twenty days for this earth-laden woman and to prove he may love her.

She has the most receptive embrace and the holiest hazel eyes he has ever seen. He believes in his destiny with guidance from Neptune and Helena, so he proposes to her,

"Let me have you for twenty days and if you are satisfied will you grant me twenty more?"

She rolls her curious fiery eyes behind her head for three seconds and stalls... then replies,

"But Helena told me to try twenty soldiers of love?"

Proteus reacts sarcastically,

"Well, in that case, why not forty?" Laughing... he continues,

"Brianna, I have traveled the underworld and the golden coast for years seeking the perfect maid and have not yet felt an embrace like yours."

Brianna receives his proclamation and smiles with a raised eyebrow. He continues his pursuit.

"Shall we dare to engage with this enchanting opportunity from Neptune and Helena in the land of Greece regardless of her tragedies?"

Proteus furthers his philosophical love chant,

"Surely you know not to tempt fate. This mission has been directed by Poseidon, god of the sea, where love flows in the valleys and back and out to the Pacific and coast-to-coast."

Brianna reciprocates and remains loyal to her counsel,

"I wouldn't want to mess with Poseidon's suggestion or command, but I must also take heed of Helena's counsel to date, twenty suitors."

Proteus pauses for a few seconds and repositions himself,

"Lady Helena stems from the hot middle earth and you are here with me now in this rejuvenating spring. Let us begin our mission, fulfill our destiny and if you are not satisfied in twenty days then I will return to the sea, my steamy goddess."

Amused and delighted, her eyes roll back down to a half smile, and she agrees,

"OK gallivant soldier, follow me."

Brianna remembers the blue cave back in the islands near the old lava tubes and decides to give this one a try here in Helena. She grabs Proteus' hand and pulls him underwater at the end of the pool near the mountainside. They swim forty feet underwater and pop up in a brilliant, iridescent blue cave with a huge air pocket above and some large rocks to rest on. Much of the sulfur gas is vented up near the cracks in the ceiling above the cave.

Brianna finds a mini blue pool in the cave. She embraces Proteus on his shoulder, clenches his arm and guides him into the purple pool. She jumps onto his torso and wraps her legs around him as she does on her surfboard. She slides her hands under his arms and embraces him firmly, planting a solid kiss on his lips. He closes his eyes as turbulent warmth radiates from his tail fin upward. Purple bubbles rise to the surface as his fin begins to shrink. He glances down and notices the transformation beginning...

Brianna squeezes tighter and kisses him again. Consequently, his tail is disappearing, and a large stump is exposed for a few seconds and then it splits into two and differentiates into two muscular legs like those of a Roman soldier.

Proteus marvels at his new land legs and recalls his experience, seeing Roman soldiers in the wars that took place in Greece and Italy. He stares in awe for five long minutes and tries standing up but realizes he's in a cave pool.

Brianna's eyes light up with stars as she feels like she's won over a unicorn but quickly realizes she must get them out of the pool and back on land to celebrate Proteus' new legs. She pulls him out of the mini pool and back into the larger cave pool and guides him,

"Kick your legs in half circles and squeeze them together to propel yourself without your large fin. Do it over and over until we get onto land. Like this." She demonstrates the breaststroke kick, and he follows.

They swim back out from the cave and back onto the spring shore with an orange and yellow crust.

Proteus stands for a brief second in ankle-high water and then trips forward and falls on his face. Brianna helps him up. He tries it again and falls again.

"I feel like I'm stuck on top of two wobbly spears." He describes.

Brianna reassures and encourages him,

"Just go slow and try it again."

He finally finds his balance and shuffles up on the dirt. He wiggles his toes in the dirt,

"This feels like crushed coral and sea chalk," he describes, trying to explain these new terrestrial sensations.

They spend the whole day learning to walk and resting under the spring geysers that shoot up into the air. Proteus keeps putting his feet in the geyser, chuckling at his new tingling feet and legs.

The next morning, Proteus climbs up a rock near the geyser where they camp out for the night. He presses down onto the hard-jagged surface and triumphantly proclaims,

"Brianna, today shall be the day one of our twenty-day adventures!" Let us begin.

He slips a little and catches himself before tumbling to the bottom into her arms. She scratches her head and suggests,

"Now that you know how to walk, let's go on a bike ride up the valley of Helena through the vineyards of her finest white grapes."

Proteus smiles and agrees,

"Yes, and we must acquire some of Helena's finest wine to give to Poseidon for his excellent guidance." She laughs and replies.

"I know where to go."

Brianna drags Proteus to the entrance of the springs where she intends to rent a double-seated bike for the afternoon. Proteus observes her pull some wet dollar bills out of her board shorts. He remembers he promised her silver drachmas if she took him to the springs.

"Brianna, I lost my silver drachmas in the cave transformation yesterday!" I promised you three silver drachmas.

"That's right. I have been so excited with our enchanting new discovery that I forgot you would lose whatever was in your fin pouch." She realizes...

"I will swim back and recover it so we can sell it in St. Helena." They walk back to the shore near the cave entrance and Brianna dives back down to retrieve the silver drachmas. She returns shortly and they begin their first land date. Brianna makes sure to secure Proteus on the back seat and instructs him to pedal along with her in circles like kicking breaststroke in the cave pool. He figures it out and they are on their way.

They ride up the vineyard in the afternoon. Dancing vines intertwine their minds.

Proteus watches Brianna's golden hair blowing in the wind while Chardonnay grapes open their blossoms as they pedal through the fields along the rows of plump white grapes.

Proteus breathes in deeply and comments,

"It smells like sea-cucumber and salad."

Brianna shares new senses with him,

"You are smelling the blossoms with your nose. To me, it smells like pares and flowers. Those are the grape blossoms."

Proteus has the confidence of a victorious knight and believes he is fulfilling his lifelong love quest. *He will love her through the tides and during many moon changes through the centuries.*

They ride up to the top of the vineyard and get off their bikes and nestle down under the wine barrels in the shade. As the afternoon light begins to dim, they gaze up into the sky and see an incredible eclipse forming a brilliant orange ring around the fading sun, allowing them to gaze in awe for minutes. The oceans, valleys, and skies unlock the curse of Proteus and open nineteen more dates for Brianna.

They drink sweet Chardonnay into the sunset, surfing moment by moment in the valley of Helena where quests are tangible, and dates begin.

They drink of love until the morning light peeks out from above the hills

Day one down, and nineteen more to go...

DISARMING EL CABRON

Friends told me when you adventure to Baja, you want to drive a crappy old car and let your hair grow out. Also, avoid shaving and grow a beard and downplay anything of value. The landscape doesn't appear as I imagine. I envision a greener landscape with point breaks around every corner. This is desolate desert, dusty and endless. It seems to go on and on to the horizon. Not too different from the landscape in *Mad Max* with Mel Gibson.

The roads slant away from the natural flow of driving where my truck feels like it's about to roll over. We keep driving through a wasteland and after about an hour from our destination, I notice a white van pull up from behind. It looks like an old van maybe from the early 80s. The van passes us and as it drives around the front of my dusty grey 1983 Toyota 4X4, I see "**FEDERALE**" in bold on the back of the van.

Buffalo prepped us for the trip and recommended we stash $20 bills in various places in the cabin of the truck.

"If the FEDERALES pull us over, we'll just give them $20 and hopefully they'll go away," reminded Buffalo.

Buffalo has been down here several times and is wise for his young years. He speaks the language and has a sophisticated vocabulary, especially for a surfer. He got his nickname from a pact he and Boxer made when they spent a whole summer sleeping in an old beat-up Buick in a buffalo field in Hanalei, Kauai. It was an affordable way to spend the summer in the nations most expensive state and still ride the best waves in the South Pacific. At the end of the summer, they branded their memories by getting tattoos of buffaloes on their ankles.

"I'm glad I have this old beat-up Toyota 4-wheel drive" I shared. It was the best $5900 I ever spent.

And Buffalo added, "and not to mention these mangy beards on our faces."

"I know what we'll do, we'll pray in Spanish!" I exclaimed.

Buffalo smiled with an amusing smirk. My nerves entertained him because I hadn't experienced anything like this before.

"Dios Mio," My God, be with us as we journey on this surf adventure.

"Gracias por una vida fina and mucho amor." Thank you for a nice life and much love!

After praying for about ten minutes, the FEDERALE dropped back behind us and eventually disappeared.

We stop in a port town about an hour and a half from the border and for the first time ever I can enjoy an authentic taco. The tacos are fresh with crunchy cabbage and a sweet aftertaste. The fish is deep fried with a batter like what I had experienced previously but this tortilla is smaller and has a sweet crunchy kind of a taste that I really enjoy. Buffalo mentioned we should slam a Corona to kill any bacteria involved with these tacos.

"Take a look Hammer, outside that harbor is one of the premier big waves here in North America" Buffalo proclaimed.

He continued to describe how big swells build from the west and the south and march to this harbor to wedge up like giant mountains of turquoise and jade that any big wave surfer would charge.

After chilling for a while near the harbor we jumped back in the car and caravanned further south for the next half an hour or so. We come up to a roadblock with four soldiers in camouflage holding machine guns. They watch us slowly drive through to our destination. As we pass them, my heart flutters a bit, as I haven't seen this before on land. The only other time was when my father and I went on a fishing trip down here on the coast. The Navy boarded our charter boat scanning routinely for drugs.

We drove on for another hour or so keeping my eyes peeled on this strangely banked road making sure the truck went forward. We approached a very tiny village, and the smell of onions permeated the air. This reminds me of Gilroy.

Buffalo motioned for me to take a right near the onion fields. I cruise down the dusty road, heading west, and few of the Vaqueros in the back of pick-up trucks are flipping us off. Buffalo says to just keep driving forward as you sometimes see this. Do we continue along the dirt road a little rattled and I marvel at how these crops can grow with so little water? This isn't Cali with abundant green artichoke and brussel sprout crops.

We drive to the end of the dirt road and pull up to the point break. It's as if we just entered a time capsule and pulled up to Pleasure Point fifty years ago. I remember seeing landscape pictures of Santa Cruz in the 1950s and 60s that were hanging in older restaurants on the wharf.

On our arrival, there are glassy head high rights rolling through with similar sections to the Point. Up here on the cliff are no roads or houses, just a dusty bluff, a dirt road, and places to camp. We even have some warmer fog present, not quite the nip like Santa Cruz, but nevertheless...fog.

Both cars pull up in anticipation of the surf. Boxer yells out,

"Hey look, we got a shoulder high swell and it's not bad. Let's hit it."

Boxer is always the most excited to charge the waves and motivate the group.

Currently my hips are bothering me, so I decide to be a team photographer. I purchased a small disposable waterproof camera. 'I had a lot of fun using these to take barrel shots at 14th Ave when we were bodysurfing and snapping pictures of endless beach-slamming barrels. One time, Johnny Boy and I even decided to pull a *wing-wave*, as I call them, and shoot barrels right at each other (left and right) and snap photos of us sliding right into each other in the close-out section. We eventually got tired of eating sand sandwiches, so we took a break from the activity for a while.'

I capture a few sweet shots of Buffalo carving the upper lips of these southern waves like a pilgrim carving a turkey on Thanksgiving. I also manage to grab an unusual photo of Boxer doing a Jack–in–the–box pop up through the roof of a barrel, a very rare occurrence in the surfing world.

After a long day of crowd-free surfing, we change, get comfortable, and plant ourselves around a warm campfire. The Lion is preparing some dinner, and Otto is pouring tequila for the boys. Our bellies warm and bliss fills our heads. Now we can relax and anticipate the days to come. As we begin settling, a white Chevy truck pulls up at the edge of the field and a man steps out intently looking our way.

He creeps out of the onion fields like a disheveled possum after a long night. He's wearing a red and grey flannel shirt with a vaquero style hat and farming boots. He's holding what appears to be a gun. He walks toward us and spins his pistol around like cowboys in the old West. He stares strangely at us with a non-verbal, "what you are doing here on my property?" type of gesture.

We all look at each other and wonder what is he doing here? My feet are just starting to warm up and I'm diving into my second anchovies, cheese, and cracker appetizer. I glance at Buffalo, and he returns curious glances back to each of us. I wondered if this man is the owner of the fields or maybe a worker or someone... communicating that he didn't want us here. No one else is here on the cliff so maybe he scared away all the other surfers and campers?

He approaches our camp and walks around the fire spinning his gun repeatedly. He has the presence like he owns the bluff and the beach and demands payment and recognition.

He circles three times (really felt like 3 hours) when I ask Otto and Buffalo if we should offer him a shot of tequila. They nod and reply, "Yep, great idea."

Buffalo offers, "Quire's tequila?"

El Cabron does not reply but glances in a yes fashion and sits down, still staring through our circle with a collective, mysterious gaze.

Otto pours him a decent size shot of Don Julio and hands him the glass. He downs the shot in one swoop and smirks a sort-of-smile. We feel some relief and continue with our appetizers. I notice the frequency of his pistol spinning begins to slow and now feel more comfortable.

Beside the fire, the Lion jumps to action and sets up a makeshift kitchen on a big piece of driftwood with the shape of a small table. It's about 5 feet across and somewhat flat. To our amazement and I'm sure to the cabrons, he spreads out 20 tortillas overlapping each other across the length of the makeshift table. He adds refried beans, lettuce, tomatoes, and when he adds the onions, *El Cabron finally smiles*. We all sigh with relief and reciprocate with big nods. The Lion pulls an ace out of his pocket and makes a five-foot-long burrito that blows the hat off *El Cabron*. He smirks, smiles, and drools. The Lion slices up the giant burrito into sections that are edible and brings one over to our undesirable friend. He chows down. Otto obliges and supplies him with another shot. The mood is easing up.

I decided to top it off by pulling out the harmonica and blowing some smooth notes his way...I play the only song I know in Spanish and sing in a celebratory mariachi sensation, "Brincan y bailan, los peces en el rio" (Swimming and dancing, the fishes in the river).

We all pulled out our best to appease this guy and it worked temporarily at least. We are all hopeful he is satisfied and will leave soon.

That night was the worst sleep of my life as I woke up every hour wondering if *El Cabron* was going to steal our stuff or kick us off the bluff. Looking back now I think he was looking to collect rent in his own personal way. He probably didn't own any land but felt it his right to tax a few surfers on adventures in his home territory.

We enjoy two more days of wonderful point break waves and leave confident that we could return and pay an unwanted visit to our less than a desirable friend. All it will take is sharing tequila, some rare and unusual dishes, and world-class music to disarm *El Cabron.*

BLUE BEAK

When Pat grew up, he worked his way out of the glades to the Gulf by feeding on a variety of fish and vegetation but seemed to have the most luck with bluegill and blueberries along the waterways and lagoons. He and his parents migrated here from Patagonia a few years ago when their local forests were being eaten by a fungus called, "Mal de Cipres." The fungus' voracious appetite for Cypress trees caused many Patagonian eagles to migrate elsewhere looking for better shelter. Because Pat was used to feeding on maqui blueberry pies in his homeland, he naturally gravitated toward the bluer, finer foods here in the Glades. As a result, he developed an iridescent blue beak over the years.

Baldwin and Betty have a perch high up in a pine tree on the coast of Marco Island on the edge of the mangroves. After a few hours of diving for grouper, Baldwin returns to their nest.

"Betty, I am not sure where all the groupers are today, but I had a 'hoot of a time' trying to catch anything out there this morning. I probably did twenty dives but came up empty-handed."

"Ok Baldi, why don't you chill with the youngins, and I'll give it a try. They could use some daddy time anyway; they've been pecking away at my feet for a while here…"

Betty swoops down off the homestead and circles above the currents by the groves on the west side near Treet Island. Sometimes the groupers swim the currents near the charter boats. She catches some swirling with her eyes and streamlines into a feathery bullet, shooting down toward the currents. She tucks her yellow beak into her white neck and torpedoes into the Gulf, targeting a grouper. She comes up with nothing. She tries again but has no luck.

Betty decides to try another mangrove inlet on the west side of Treet Island. She lands on an old boating shack with old kayaks and runs down dingy boats. There is a nice ripping current curving around the island west and south. Out of the east, a large male eagle dives toward her like a speeding bullet except Betty can't see his beak. It's as if he is a fast phantom diving out of the sky. No yellow beak just swift, mysterious, and fast. He shoots through the water with a little splash and pops up with a nice grouper. He flies it over to the sand and lands to tear it apart. Betty looks closer and barely sees his beak.

She waits for him to finish eating, as all eagles know not to encroach on each other's catch. Top predators have unspoken territories and general boundaries. After finishing off his kill, he glides over to the east side of Treet Island near the palm trees with a few dehydrated coconuts on the sand underneath. He tears off the top of the fibrous coconut, cleaning his mysterious beak.

Betty lifts off and flies over to his side of the beach and lands next to him. She skips and lifts, and skips a couple times over to him and asks,

"Excuse me, nice dive, earlier! I saw you catch that grouper with ease in that westerly current. May I ask, what happened to your beak?"

"Haw, ha" You Goldies are funny, you expect every eagle on earth to have bright yellow beaks." Pat chuckles.

"I am a Patagonian Eagle and have a blue beak from years of munching on maqui berries and, I loved it there, but a vicious fungus called the "Mal De Cipres" took over and started eating the trees. So, we migrated here to the Gulf as we heard of all the abundance of fish and berries up here."

"Wow, can I take a closer look? Betty curiously leans in toward the mysterious predator.

"How cool and amazing, I've never seen a blue beak eagle..."

Pat smiles and shares confidently,

"We have a hit rate five times the golden eagle when diving for grouper. I've counted.

I think our blue beaks blend in with the water and give us that extra edge to snag em inconspicuously"

Betty twists her neck and nods,

"That must be why we have been having a harder time lately."

"Golden's have to try five times as hard and not to mention, the grouper schools haven't been running as much this spring."

Betty nods, "That makes sense on why we have had trouble catching our normal grouper."

Pat adds, "Yep, that and your giant yellow beacons alarming the fish that you're diving in to snag them."

Betty laughs curiously but is still concerned for her family,

"What should we do?"

Pat opens his wings for a flap or two letting some air onto his belly and exhaling out a big breath.

"I know," he smoothly chirps, "Let's go berry hunting! Meet me at the base of the glades, over by ten lakes and I'll show you where the bundles of berries are."

"Okay," Betty agrees and lifts and off Treet Island and flaps against the wind and finds a drift air current pulling her into the ten lakes area. She spiral focuses down on the edge of the Everglades and sees a warm spot in her vision where the dense humid jungle meets the salty ocean. She drops her head and wings follow into a descent. She sees Pat on a wooden pole near the water's edge.

"Over here," Pat directs Betty.

"Land near the inlet water brush over on the inland side where that sandy embankment is open." He reassures.

Pat lands first, then Betty. On the easterly ocean side there is a large pool of wading water but on the westerly jungle side is a huge bush of glade blueberries.

"This is a nice bundle here," Pat encourages.

"Wow, what beautiful blue colors!" Betty exclaims.

"Come on Goldie, dig in!"

Betty pulls a few off the bush and twists and jerks her bright beacon of a yellow beak.

"Mmm, sweet and fibrous." An iridescent blue begins to speckle on her beak.

"Eat more," Pat continues.

After five more berry grabs, Betty's beak is completely covered in blue and stained nicely over the brilliance of gold that once radiated from her head.

"I feel so sticky and pasty but excited at the same time."

Pat hops over and chuckles at her blue Patagonian like beak.

"I think one more will do the trick and seal the deal," he confirms.

"Okay" Betty dives into one more bush and seals over her weapon with total blue.

"Awesome, let's fly back out to Treet Island" Pat suggests.

Betty lifts off and follows Pat to Treet Island. She wonders what Baldwin would think of her sailing along with a mysterious blue *male* eagle from the exotic southern tip of South America but continues along on the fun adventure.

Five minutes later they approach Treet Island and catch a downward drift onto the easterly side. Pat diverts quickly to the currents, streamlines his dive and parts the surface effortlessly and comes up with a three-pound grouper.

Betty caught up in the thrill, darts right a few hundred feet past Pat and dives for one herself. Armed with extra confidence, she attacks the currents like a blue phantom in the night. She pulls the dive, breaks the surface smoothly, and comes up with a five-pound grouper.

"Nice catch!" Pat applauds.

"That felt awesome. You got me sold on this "blue beak" thing." Betty exclaims.

"Thank you for sharing your secret hunting tactics with me. I will return to the nest and feed the youngins."

"No problem," Pat replies.

"And let me know if your male chap wants a lesson."

Betty clenches the fresh hefty grouper and lifts off to fly back to her home. On the way back, she ponders how she is going to explain her blue-stained beak to Baldwin.

IN THE MANGROVES

As I step foot on the pancake battered sand, I sink deep into the powdery earth. Tiger tail shells scatter in the sand softly with their red-orange color beaming brightly enough to compete with sunrise shells in Kauai. Their yellow ridges fan out, resembling a brilliant setting sunset. Each one having slightly different colors radiating from orange to fuschia hues. My favorite shells have a spray effect with powdery rusty red paintbrush outlining the ridges of the Tiger tails.

Outside the shallow sandbar, bull sharks chase grouper fish into the fisherman's nets where they bravely shuffle the sands at knee-high water level. wonder why no one is swimming in the tiny waves of the shallows? After scanning the whole beach, I see maybe one or two walkers wading in the shoreline at ankle water level.

I gaze past the fisherman's cast and see waves of whitewash spraying out from the sides of the black Water Ninja. The winding sound of the engine quiets down and a bronze, tan woman scans the shores where I was beachcombing.

I am checking out this colorful hermit crab with a cool rainbow swirl around its spiral when I pop up and notice the tan beauty parking the Ninja right up on the sand next to me. What was she doing? She jumped off the *black water beast* and strolled over to me swinging her arms confidently. She swaggers, side to side, like a curvy model on a runway.

Her hazel gems radiate Ibeauty that penetrate light into my iris' and up my optic nerve, shooting nerve signals straight to my parietal lobe where my brain feels like prey being hunted. I felt like a grouper in a Bull sharks' mouth but kind of liked it. I gladly jump up to engage and she blurts out,

"Hey, I saw you on shore with those obviously obnoxious bright orange shorts and thought you could help me. Anyone who can wear those in public can't be afraid of a little adventure, haw?

"Have you been to the mangroves where the manatee swim and the eagles fly and nest?"

Hesitantly, I replied, "No, I didn't even know they were there." She grabs my arm and pulls me over to the *water ninja.*

"I need your help, I lost something very valuable and need you to help me find it."

We both push the *Ninja* out into the water. She crawls up and straddles the machine like a cowgirl on a stallion and prompted me, "Jump on!" So, I straddle her bodacious backside and cup up against this warm woman with cold, beaded water droplets on her curvy rump. I feel like a chick jumping on a man's Ninja Road bike, *silly... but this was exciting.*

She hits the throttle and planes out smoothly at about 25 mph. We start gliding forward like a magic carpet ride. We are floating and gliding on the surface of the mysterious Gulf of Florida. As we pass the first bend in the groves, she points up to the eagle's nest where dad is chilling in the nest and mom is completing her full circle to land with freshly caught grouper and mullet. She emphasizes that the father eagle is watching the eaglets while mom is finishing a hunt.

"What are we looking for?" I ask.

"Just wait, you'll see." She replies.

We motor around two more curves in the mangroves that open into little coves surrounded by woody, twining roots the size of tree branches that have big lattice structures you would never want to get caught in.

I began to realize my doom... She probably wants me to jump into these crazy, woody maze-like weeds in the sea to find something.

'How the hell am I going to do this, *she is hot*, and I don't want to let her down?'

She slows the beast down to about 10 mph and slides back into my groin where I feel a *well of bells ring* and *waves of warm water* shoot through my core.

Her hair is a smoky amber color with strands of gold and highlights of crimson streaking on the bangs. Her wet hair is beaded with twists and knots and salty strands peppering into dread-like clumps. We hit a bump in the water and her skin reverberates like set waves on a golden California evening surf session. Her skin waves boomerang back up through her abdomen as I watch them roll through her back section and then *"Whoa"* ... I notice a sweet looking red Hawaiian hibiscus flower tattoo showing through her black lattice bathing suit. This is feeling very familiar to me now. I want to squeeze and caress her plump backside but wait patiently. My curiosity arouses, as I look closer through the diamond cut on her black silky suit. Red velvet with foamy, frothy espresso comes to mind. We hit a wake and I clench onto her sides. My desperate hands slip down her sides and slither through the Hawaiian Tropic sunblock glazed on her back. The coconut smell reminds me of the *Sandwich Islands* and makes me wonder if the palm trees on the shore here could have produced the coconuts in the sexy lotion on her body. We hit another bump and she reach around with her left hand to see if I was still on. Her strongly exquisite hand feels like warm electricity through my left leg.

'Will I get the prize? What was in store for me?'

She pulls the *Water Machine* up to a smaller outlet in the groves around three corners and pleads with me to help her find a gold coin that she lost near the outlet.

"While I was on an island near the 13 markers, I found a Spanish Reale sparkling in the shallow sand, and while I was returning to Marco beach, I hit a wake from an outside boat and the bump launched my gold coin somewhere over there by the groves...

If you retrieve it for me, I will take you to Treet Island, a place you will never forget!" Excitement swirled in my loins and mind. The mystery took over and I became fearless. Maybe my dorky loud, bright orange board shorts will get me some love treasure after all.

She opens the hatch in between our legs and pulls out a mask. She throws it my way. *What the hell, sharks don't like mangroves right, the groves are just too convoluted and woody, so the worst I could run into would be a manatee or barracuda right?*

I strap on the diving mask and submerge my face in the water and see jade pastel-colored water. I must grab onto something to get down lower. These groves must be about thirty feet deep... I weave down a woody grove a few more feet down and see just more and more lattices to the murky bottom. I come back up to grab a breath and then try again. I weave and swirl down the maze slipping and sliding around these roots in the sea. Suddenly I feel a slap on my right thigh. I come up and see a manatee surfacing. I was just bitch-slapped by a mama manatee watching over her little whale. I wonder if she saw my awesome shorts and thought I was a threat? Ok, I'll try again... I dive down again and go another ten feet and see more sand and green leafy outgrowths on the roots. I have no idea how I'm supposed to make it to the bottom. I can't even see past ten feet or so.

As I surface up for air, a sharp vice-script bite slams me down on my side near my right gluteal. *'I hope that was a Barracuda.'* My right side was exposed out to the side away from the groves, so I quickly jump deeper into the groves more toward the middle where all the thick bushes are. I wedge myself in between two trees so whatever it is, won't get me again. Then, the green jade color turns blood red. A shark or something must have hit me? But I still have my arms and legs intact, thank God!

I heard the *Water Ninja* start up again and see a small fin surface and swim out away from us back out to sea. It must have been a bull or a mangrove shark if they exist?

Wonder woman grabs me and pulls me up onto the deck of the black beast and gives me a rash guard and instructs me to put pressure on my wound and hold it there.

"I will get us out of here." She screams.

She hits the throttle and planes out in between the mangroves. I hold on tightly with my left arm around her waist and simultaneously pressing firmly with my rash guard onto my right side. I bravely lift the rash guard to gauge the severity of the cut and thank GOD it was about three to four shark teeth wide but not huge.

"I am so sorry," she regretfully sighs...I saw the bull snag one of the trees and your side too. I think you will be fine because the cuts look small."

I am so happy he only nicked you on your side. I am so sorry! I will take care of you."

I held on to her for what seemed like for hours but was probably only fifteen minutes. She pulls up to this white sandy island with palm trees and a little shack. She rushes me over to the shack and opens an emergency kit with these big clear adhesives strips and glues my lacerations together.

"They're STERIS trips, you will be fine. You are so lucky he only got three teeth in, or we'd be screwed."

She walks me over to a hammock between two palm trees and has me wait for her to return,

She brings me back some coconut water, an emergency kit and stitches me up. I wrap my hands around her curves that I gazed upon hours and ponder...

"Am I a sucker for this woman's love?"

She commands me to chill in the hammock for a few and then goes down to the water next to the edge of the groves and brings back some blue crabs and more coconuts.

She cracks the coconut open with a rock and then peels the shell off the crab and gives me cracked crab and coconut sushi style. Maybe this was all worth the adventure.

"I am so sorry, but you are the only guy I figured would try and help me." I owe you my life," she proclaims.

"No worries," I reassure her.

"I guess I am a sucker for danger. I was getting little-bored hunting seashells anyway."

She laughed.

"Here, try some of this Treet Island Rum."

She pours some in a half coconut shell and I drink, and sooth, and drink more. My insides warm up and my teeth and gums get numb. She takes a swig too.

"I like drinking rum" she shares with me. "If you have a couple of these you will feel better and forget about what happened."

"Do you want me to take you back to Marco Island beach after your drink, I feel horrible."

"No, I am ok." After all this, I think we should chill for a while" ... I felt comfortable with the Water Woman Ninja lady.

She agrees and then presses her soft salty lips against mine...

Coconut, watery, rum bliss fills my core from my teeth to my lips, to my stomach. I think to myself I would do this all again for a kiss from Water Ninja Woman. She puts her hands on my lower back and rubs my soft spot above my gluteus.

I am pretty sure the bright orange board shorts attracted both Wonder woman and the shark, but to tell you the truth, I would do this all over again. What an awesome day! Tomorrow I will wear my silver board shorts...

ACKNOWLEDGEMENTS

This book is dedicated to those who dare to imagine and utilize creativity in their daily practice of life. A special thanks to my wife and daughters who consistently tolerate my endless chatter and comments about my writings.

CREDITS

Around the Wall, *Atherton Review*, April 2021.

Jade Cove, *October Hill Magazine*, spring, 2022.

Malady Mahi, *New English Review*, June 2020.

Maize of Color, *Short Edition*, July 2020, Community Winner of the America, color it in contest.

Of Song & Stitches, *Rigorous Mag*, Volume 4, Issue 3.

Opposition, *Route 7 Review*, December 2019.

The Put-Back, *Forbidden Peak Press*, July 2019.

ABOUT THE AUTHOR

Tony Martello is a storyteller like no other—a family therapist by day and a masterful weaver of short fiction by night. He's the creative force behind *Flat Spell Tales, Under The Curtain,* and *Of Song & Stitches,* with all three brought vividly to life on Audible. His evocative stories have found homes in renowned publications like *October Hill Magazine, New English Review, Atherton Review,* and *Short Edition.* When he's not crafting compelling narratives, Tony enjoys life in scenic San Luis Obispo, CA with his wife and daughters.